Love & Radio in the Time of the Apocalypse

By Lydia Joy

Love & Radio in the Time of the Apocalypse

Published by Ink And Quill Press, 2026

For more excellent works of fiction, visit Inkandquillpress.com

Cover artwork by Lydia Joy

I: BETWEEN

'Tis with him in standing water, between boy and man.

-Shakespeare, *Twelfth Night*

1: STATIC

When Jo found the radio inside the old outpost, she wasn't sure what it was at first. All she knew was that the tiny, gray box was noisy. Its hiss ripped through the rafters of the cabin, and if she didn't shut it up, it would draw every biter in the area like ants to honey.

It wasn't that she was too young to remember the old world, she was six when people started turning. She remembered classrooms, family trips to the beach, and devices adults turned on for noise or voices. She'd had a smaller one as a kid, more like a toy, and used it to whisper secrets to the boy next door.

Jo picked up the box. It was covered in knobs and, when turned, emitted an ear-splitting ring. She almost dropped it in surprise, and fumbled with the many dials until, at last, it went quiet.

Her heart hammered in her ears. Jo closed her hand around the knife at her hip.

Something rustled outside the cabin. A shape pushed through a rotting hole in the wall, splintering wood as it came.

A woman. Or what had been one. Her eyes were fogged over and her skin held the color of spoiled milk. A ring marked her throat where she'd been bitten. Roots spilled from the wound, yellow and curling, threading around her arms and legs, pulling her forward.

Jo ducked as the woman swiped at her. For a split second, something stupid surfaced: a puppet show she'd seen one once, long ago, at the beach.

She remembered a boardwalk under her feet and sand grinding under her sneakers. She could almost smell butter in the salty air. If she concentrated hard enough, she could see bursts of color over the dark ocean, too bright to belong to night.

Fireworks. That was the word.

The woman gurgled and lunged again.

Jo sidestepped. One biter she could handle. More than one, maybe not, not if the noise box had carried. So, she did what she'd been taught. Her boot came down on the back of the woman's knee. Bone gave way with a wet crack. Jo drove her dagger into the skull and didn't stop until the body sagged forward.

The smell hit her late. Rot. Sweet and wrong. It never failed to turn her stomach.

The box rattled in her grip. Something loose knocked around inside as she turned it over, fingers tracing the shallow grooves in the plastic. She found a tiny door on the back and pried it open.

A scrap of paper slipped into her palm.

For a moment, she thought it might be a cigarette. The Wolfskins used to roll them until they ran out of paper. But upon closer inspection, she could see printed words, ink bleeding. She unrolled it and held it right against her eye, wondering how a person had managed to draw that small. A cluster of circles, a winding line, and a wide square centered on the scrap.

Her first thought was *map*, and she pocketed it.

As she turned to leave, Jo stopped. She looked back at the biter's face, which was already deflating as the brain died. The shape staring back at her was familiar.

The woman's name was Ruth. Or, it used to be. Jo stared into the empty eye sockets as yellow flowers threaded through what was left of her friend's body, and wished she'd never known what had happened to her.

Shaken, Jo brought the gray box back to the gates of Burning Well. She submitted to protocol. The gatekeeper ran his hands over her neck, her ribs, her arms, tugged at her clothes to check for tears or blood. No one needed to be reminded what had happened the last time an infected person had slipped past the walls.

He barely glanced at the box on her belt. Jo was always bringing back trash, old-world junk no one wanted. When he declared her clean, the iron gates opened.

Jo ran all the way home.

She placed the box into Rafael's dark, roughened hands. His tired eyes sharpened, then brightened, like fireworks.

"We won't tell the General about this one," he said.

2: MIC CHECK

RADIO LOG 01
Location: Ambridge

[A click]

[Papers rustling]

[An inhale and exhale]

A VOICE: …llo? Helloooo? Testing, testing, 1-2-3…that's working, right? Kind of. Lalala. Red leather, yellow leather. Irish wristwatch. Iwish Wristratch.

Hm. Okay.

Just gonna play it back, make sure it's recording…

[Rustling]

[A click]

3: IT WORKS

RADIO LOG 02
Location: Ambridge

[Click]

A VOICE: Holy crap, it worked. This is crazy. I literally don't believe it. It. Worked. It works! Haha! I'm a genius.

Hi! Hey! Hello to whoever is listening, or I guess whoever will be listening to this recording later on if that's a possibility. Wowie. Okay. Focus. At the time of recording, it's March 17th, 2029, pretty sure. We try to keep track of that. My name is Ezra.

EZRA [cont]: Originally, I thought I'd just play around with the radio here, but then I kept playing around until I accidentally got it working. "Accidentally," like I haven't been here fiddling with it for days.

Currently, I'm recording from the old Ambridge Radio Station. Man, you should have seen the state of the place when I broke in here. I had to break in since Birdie had roped it off for years, but she couldn't stop your boy. It was totally boarded up, all covered in moss and debris and *so* many spiders. When I broke through one of the windows and landed inside, there was something way worse than spiders growing in there.

I really should have put two and two together. I was way too excited to get my grubby little hands on all the tech that I'd dropped *right* into a biter nest. Four of them, growing out of the walls, dragging themselves around, with those gross yellowy vines comin' out of their noses and eyeballs—*eugh*.

Really stupid of me, I'll own that. But Theo came to my rescue—I guess older brothers are good for something. He even helped me get rid of the old crew and clean the place up a bit. He was pissy about it the whole time, but, hey, at least no one got bit. So chill. Birdie wasn't even that mad when I told her about breaking into the radio station. Better to ask forgiveness than permission, right?

So now you, future listener, can see in your mind's eye what life was like here in Ambridge.

That's the town. Ambridge. Birdie says it was in a state when they first got here—she's one of our leaders, I guess. Badass, ex-military. We've got gardens, a barn, some horses, which I'm too scared to get close to, and we're still working on getting the electricity running throughout. I'm doing most of that; only got shocked once. We're a work in progress, but it's come a long way since Birdie picked me and my brother up those years back.

This is a nice little spot away, though. A big room, all to myself.

We've replaced the windows and, obviously, fixed some loose beams, and all that. It's been a good side project when I'm not on scout duty. I'm not so good with a gun, but Birdie wants us all to learn.

The radio tower here is not in good shape. At all. It's rusted to all heck, and it's missing a limb, which I guess is crucial to the structural integrity or something. I may be safe from biters in here, but that doesn't mean I'm safe from my own hubris.

But there is good news. I was sweeping out the station this morning and found this loose plank on the floor. A pretty good hidey-hole, since it took me a few days to find it. I don't like sticking my hands in holes on a good day, as raccoons are pretty high on the list of things to be wary of. But there wasn't a raccoon hiding in the hole, dear listener.

Inside there was a box, and it was full of spools of wire and handheld radios and batteries? I'm talking about the rechargeable kind, y'know with the panels you just leave out in the sun? And duct tape, which as we all know, is the most powerful survival tool in existence. And I've been hankering for a good set of pliers. And there was that headset I was asking for. Makes it easy to talk hands-free.

[A shuffle]

EZRA [distantly]: I know you can't see me right now, but I'm currently taking a stroll around the room. Why, hello, south wall…And well, well, hello, north wall.

[Another shuffle]

EZRA [cont.]: Can you imagine how much easier it'll be to keep in contact while we're out scouting? Much less hassle to call than it is to scream across town that your leg's getting eaten by biters.

…Hm, that was too dark, huh? Sorry. I only said it because that's something that happened kind of recently so it was in my brain.

Anyway, this all hinges on if we can get the tower to stand on its own. I think that's step one. I'd have to get Birdie excited about it, but if I can fix the tower, clean up the walkie-talkies, and get a signal going…

…I think we can use this.

[Click]

4: RUTH

Smoke billowed in plumes against a dark sky. The scent of fire cut through the winter air. Jo strained her ears. Nothing answered but an owl.

"Burning," Nell said at her side. She leaned over the cool lip of the wall and wrinkled her nose. "Wonder who got bit."

Jo tightened her grip on the rifle. She tracked the treeline, finger hovering over the smooth wood. "Hope it wasn't one of ours," Nell said. Her fingers were tangled in her dirty-blonde hair, the same hair she refused to cut, no matter how often it snagged on branches.

She rocked back on her crate, tipping so far Jo braced for the fall.

"But if someone did get offed, I mean, there's an opening on the Wolfskins now." Nell leaned farther, testing gravity. "Sienna says my aim's improving. So, hey. Could be my turn. Sucks someone died, but with her backing me—"

Jo looked at her.

"Why are you staring like that?" Nell demanded.

"B-because you're s-saying dumb s-stuff," Jo said. She shifted her grip on the rifle. The words scraped on the way out. She felt it happen and hated it.

Nell didn't flinch.

"People die every day. I was just saying. Like the bride you found in the woods. What was her name? Reba?"

"R-Ruth," Jo said.

Nell whistled.

"That's the worst. I ran into one of my teachers once. Mr. Rainier." She chewed on the end of a braid. "It's not really them anymore, I don't think, which should make it better, but I don't know if it does."

She paused, then kept going. "Sienna said she'd put in a good word for me. If I got in, I'd have to cut my hair." Nell tugged the braid, frowning. "I don't want to. But I guess that's the price."

She glanced sideways at Jo. Lantern light flickered across her pale skin. "You want to be a Wolfskin too, right?"

Jo shrugged and sighted down her rifle at a lumpy shadow moving through the narrow pines below.Biters didn't climb this high often. The cold kept most of them away. But there was always the stray.

"I see you and Rafael practicing," Nell said. "I wish they could take both of us. Then I'd actually have someone my age." She huffed. "But they'll only pick one, I know it. And you're the captain's kid, so that's already a strike against me."

Jo lowered the rifle. Even with her dad in charge, she doubted they wanted someone like her on an elite team. Someone too quiet, whose words caught and tripped. She pictured the Wolfskins in their heavy gear, looking down at her while she struggled to get a sentence out.

Nell's eyes followed the barrel as Jo aimed her weapon down at the dark treeline.

"Maybe you could teach me some of that tracking stuff. That's the only thing Sienna says I need practice with."

Jo gave a quick nod.

A figure broke from the trees, bare feet scraping through frost. Yellow curls spilled from the empty sockets where its eyes had been. Brown moss clung to its body in damp sheets, threaded through skin gone soft and pale. Air hissed out of its broken jaw as it moved, wet and uneven.

It staggered toward the gate.

Jo raised her rifle from the wall.

"What about the noise?" Nell said.

Jo waited. The biter lurched closer, close enough for her to see the small white flowers embedded across its skin. She fired.

The shot cracked through the clearing. The body dropped hard, a thin string of smoke rising from the hole between its eyes.

Another corpse for the fire. Better that than letting it reach the walls of Burning Well.

At last, an orange glow flickered through the trees. It started as small as a star and slowly grew as it approached. Heavy footfalls chorused through the woods until a weary band of people and horses halted in front of the metal gates. Jo searched the frost-bitten faces until a broad figure separated from the pack. Her shoulders slumped with relief as her dad, Rafael, looked up at her from the ground below. He unwound the scarf from around his dark, bearded face.

"One dead! None infected!" he barked up.

"You get any meat?" Nell called down. "A deer, maybe?"

"Open the gate," Rafael ordered.

"Who died?"

"Open the gate *now*, Nell."

Nell jumped to obey. As soon as the metal gate had lifted, the pack of Wolfskins marched wearily inside, minus one.

The bags under Rafael's eyes told her how the trip had gone.

Back at their cabin, Jo slid a mug across the table. The beans were ancient, closer to dirt than the old-world coffee Rafael never stopped talking about. He drank it anyway, eyes closed, his shoulders easing. "Where'd you get this?" He asked, turning the mug as if the answer might be stamped on the bottom.

"Found it," she said.

He shot her a sideways look. "Should I ask where?"

She shook her head. HQ had plenty. They wouldn't miss the handful she'd smuggled out in her pocket.

Rafael didn't press. He finished the mug and looked better for it.

He used to tell her how cabins worked in the old world. Kids packed into bunk beds stacked to the ceiling. Their place was quieter. One small bedroom for Jo and the rest divided by curtains. Rag rugs hung on the walls, sunbleached but thick enough to hold the warmth. Old tins and mismatched cups lined the shelves. The stove took up most of the space, blackened and solid, always warm.

The box wasn't out. Rafael kept it hidden in a drawer in case anyone went looking. Still, Jo knew where it was. At night, she could hear him turning the dials, the soft crackle of static leaking through the walls.

"We were jumped by some people," Rafael explained when the coffee finally woke him. "It was too much noise. The biters came fast."

"Who got b-bit?" Jo asked.

"Cecil." Rafael shook his head. "He wanted us to make it quick before he turned. We burned the body in the west hills."

Jo had to think hard to remember his face. Cecil had been like any other Wolfskin on Rafael's team: big, loud, built like a tank. It hadn't taken more than a bite for him to beg for death.

"Who a-attacked?" Jo asked, picking loose coffee grinds from under her fingernails.

"Didn't recognize them," Rafael said. "We spooked each other. That's how it goes lately." He lifted the mug again, then lowered it when he remembered it was empty. "There's not enough game to support both us and Redgrass. People get jumpy when they're hungry." He shrugged. "Other places are feeling the pressure. I warned the General, told him pushing outside of our territory would only make things worse." A tired breath left him. "But you know how he is. Always wants more ground."

Jo pressed her chapped lips together and Rafael watched her. His hand twitched on the table as if he meant to reach out.

"It's getting warmer," Rafael said instead. "Biters'll get restless."

Jo caught him changing the subject and let it pass. She nodded. "They like the rain."

"We talked about moving higher up the mountain," he went on. "Where it's cold enough that nothing grows. No biters up there."

Jo scowled at him.

"Yeah, yeah. Freeze or starve instead," Rafael said with a chuckle. "Burn through the last of the wood and call it living. And there's no one to trade with up there. No good options. It's a catch-22."

"A w-what?"

"Y'know, it's like…you lose either way. *Catch-22*, it was a book. World War II. They made us read it in high school."

"I should read it s-sometime," Jo said, half-teasing. Burning Well didn't keep books, not outside the General's house.

Rafael snorted and tipped back the empty mug. "Don't be a smartass. You would've hated high school, anyway."

The week was filled with whispers. The topic of a trade with Kettering surfaced every time there were fewer rations to pass out than the day before. When workers complained, the captains reminded them that General Hayes's household would still be eating that night.

"I bet you wish you were back in the General's house," sneered one of the boys as they walked the perimeter. "Bet you miss your cushy bed and three square meals."

Jo ignored these comments when she could, and was relieved when they reached the General's courtyard.

Her comrades liked to circle the fenced-in perimeter in the hopes of catching a glimpse of one of the brides.

"They're there," someone muttered. "On the path. The fat one and the pretty one."

"Move your head, I can't see."

Jo peeked through the bars and caught two figures circling the concrete tower. They floated along the path on bare feet, arms linked. They were wrapped in washed linen, pale against the gray. One was dark-haired and narrow, the other freckled and rounded in the middle. Far enough along that Jo felt a quiet count start in her head.

The boys pressed up to the fence, craning for a better look.

Jo shifted her bag straps and slipped around the corner of the wall. The boys weren't stupid enough to cross into the enclosure. And none of them knew about the spot where the bars bent just wide enough for someone thin to pass through.

Jo crouched at the far corner of the courtyard. She waited until the two women passed, then shoved her backpack through the gap and squeezed after it. They stopped short when they saw her.

"Johanna," said Faith, her hand resting on her belly. Snow cut off the path first, quick and close. Faith followed more carefully, one hand steadying her belly as she eased down beside the wall.

"We've been walking circles all morning," Snow said. "Thought you'd ditched us."

"She always comes," Faith said.

Jo opened the bag and Snow leaned in the second the glass showed.

"Oh." She reached for it immediately.

Faith caught her wrist. "Careful."

Snow froze, then laughed under her breath and took the bottle slower this time. "Not even cracked. This'll do perfectly for plant cuttings, or flowers."

"Do we really need more green things?" Faith said, peering into the bag. "You know what he does when he finds them."

"He barely steps into the parlor," Snow said. She tapped the bottle with her nail. "And they stay up on the sill. He won't notice." She glanced at Jo. "What other shiny things, Crow?"

Jo showed them: a set of tin cups, a handful of carved chess pieces, a broken watch with a nice leather strap, another soda bottle, and a metal lunchbox with a cartoon illustration on the front. The inks were faded a muted shade of brown, but on close inspection, it may have once been blue.

Faith tested the latch.

"Billie will love this," she said. "She's been wanting something to put her sewing in."

Snow frowned. "It's kind of big to sneak back."

Faith didn't answer. She gathered the other items, lifted her skirts, and tucked the lunchbox beneath the white fabric so it rested against her belly. It vanished, save for one sharp corner pressing out. "How's your training, Johanna?" Faith asked, shifting to keep it from knocking.

Jo nodded. "Fine enough." She glanced at Faith's middle and lifted her hand in a small question.

"Eight months," Snow said. She tipped Jo's bag and shook it, checking for anything left behind. "Then she'll be ready for another one."

Jo frowned, counting. "F-five?" she asked.

"Six," Faith said. She leaned back and stretched until her spine cracked. "And I'm hoping that's it."

Snow stiffened. "Don't say that." Her eyes flicked to the open courtyard. "Don't, Faith. You don't want them to toss you out."

Faith let out a breath and eased herself onto a low rock. Jo stepped in and steadied her. "I can't keep doing this," Faith said. "When it stops, he'll put me outside, same as Ruth."

Snow's eyes shone, bright and wet. "You'll be redeemed," she said quickly. "One of the men will want you. You just have to be good."

Faith traced a finger over the corner of the lunchbox, which poked out from under a veil of white fabric. "If the General's men are anything like him," she said, "I don't want them."

Jo swallowed.

"What's it like out there now?" Faith asked. Her smile was still there, but her eyes looked dead-set. "All he talks about are the biters and the men and the cannibals." She paused. "But there is a way to kill the biters, though. You do it all the time. And you've never been bitten."

"We shouldn't talk about that," Snow muttered, turning the glass bottle over and over in her hands.

"If it comes to it, I'll have to learn," Faith said sternly. "I could make fires once, a long time ago." She touched Jo on the shoulder.

"You could show me."

Snow hissed, low.

"And your children?"

Faith's mouth tightened. "I haven't seen them since weaning."

Jo saw the tower windows in her memory, and Faith standing there, hands on the sill, watching the street below, always looking for a child the right size, or with the same shade of hair.

The children didn't live near the tower. They trained across the city, in the barracks by the yards. Still, Faith kept an eye out.

"I should've asked Ruth how to bring one down," Faith said. She stared up at the wisps of clouds. "I hope she's all right."

Jo bit her lip, the image of Ruth's round face rushing to the front of her mind. Ruth had kept her onyx hair shaved close to the scalp, but not for ease or cleanliness. It was out of spite. The General hated it.

She'd arrived not long before Jo and slid into the house like she'd been there all along. She laughed louder than the others and talked about leaving as if it were a real plan and not a dangerous thought; said it often enough that it sounded possible.

The rest of them didn't talk like that, not even Faith. They got their warm beds, full plates, books, sometimes. A little television, if they behaved. That was the bargain.

Ruth didn't take bargains.

She searched the house when she thought no one was watching, asking the delivery men questions she wasn't supposed to ask, tugging drawers open, lifting rugs, and peering behind furniture. Once, she went into the General's room. That was a mistake.

The guards took her through the vault doors and she came back the next day, uncharacteristically quiet. Jo had never been sent out. She learned early how to keep still.

One night, Ruth showed them a door beneath the General's bed, a narrow seam in the floor. The brides crouched close, murmuring guesses about what he kept hidden from them.

Ruth said the General kept Shakespeare behind his headboard. She even stole a paperback once called *Twelfth Night.*

The words were strange, but Ruth made them sound sparkly. She said she'd played Viola in high school and talked about the night the set collapsed during Act Two, the wall of Orsino's house tipping toward her. No one stopped the show. They worked around it, joked it into the script, let the servants take the blame. The audience laughed and stood up at the end.

Ruth vanished not long after the book went missing. She was marched through the vault doors, and didn't return.

For a while, Jo told herself someone had redeemed her, too. She hoped that an elder had stepped in, like Rafael had stepped in for her. She'd hoped Ruth was somewhere warm.

Then Jo found her in the woods.

The three girls jumped as a sharp laugh carried across the courtyard.

Faith shoved the bag back into Jo's hands, quick and firm. Snow was already backing away, eyes darting to the fence.

"Go," Faith said under her breath.

Jo didn't argue. She slung the strap over her shoulder and slipped back through the gap, scraping her arms on the metal. The bars pressed in on her ribs, then released her.

On the other side, she crouched and pulled the bag close. She could have told them. She almost had.

But knowing hadn't saved Ruth. It hadn't helped anyone.

5: FOR THE RECORD

RADIO LOG 03
Location: Ambridge

EZRA: I'm back.

…

I guess I don't need to announce that. I'm the only one who records on this thing, as far as I know.

I wasn't going to keep recording, actually. The last ones were more of a test, just to make sure everything was in working order, you know. But, I dunno, it's kind of nice to have a space to observe your thoughts, and I've got a lot of those. Also, it's quieter in here than anywhere else. When I shut the door, it almost feels like things are normal, or like I don't have to worry about a biter wandering by.

Plus, Ambridge has never had records before.

Birdie says memory's a luxury. She says "you remember later, if you're lucky!" I think she's half right. But if no one remembers anything, then what are we even…doing?

I guess when you're so focused on making it through the night, there really isn't time. But since we've got the fence in place and good people and routines, well, there's wiggle room for something more, right? And, who knows? Maybe these logs will give you, dear listener, a snapshot of what life was like during the end times.

Hm, that's bleak. It can't really be the end if some of us are still here. The Hard Times? Like, when people say: "We fell on some hard times," it could just mean right now. The Really Hard Times, how about that?

Soooo, updates? Well, since you asked, I'm tinkering with the HAM radio as I sit here. I've never used one of these, and am a little cautious to see if anyone talks back. Honestly, I think the insides are too fried to actually do anything. I'm sure the previous guys tried to call someone before they kicked it.

Theo and I are getting the walkies tightened up, and with the batteries charged, they should be operational. We're giving them a test run when I get back from Roslyn.

It's so weird going to a town that's got real, functioning buildings inside of it. Roslyn is old and everything was built from stone and brick and concrete, so it's lasted the test of time. Like a cockroach. And they're organized, too. I think Birdie wishes Ambridge had it more together, but hey, we're scrappy.

Scrappy's good, too. And I feel like we're really privileged to have friendly alliances with other communities. Not everyone can say that, I'm sure.

Look at me being positive.

The best part about Roslyn is the library. That's probably the only thing I wish Ambridge had. You know, that might be the reason I keep volunteering to go on trade runs, just for the chance to get my grubby little hands on some books.

I don't think I've talked about the library yet. If these logs do anything, I want them to be a reminder that there was at least one cool thing that stood through the zombie apocalypse, and it was the Roslyn Library.

A lot of the folks working there were librarians before the Really Hard Times happened. Once it all started going down, they decided to stay and keep the library clean, safe, and available to anyone who needed it. Roslyn made a rule that you couldn't take books off the premises because they became too precious. But you could stay as long as you wanted and read or copy them. Actually, the librarians encouraged making copies so that the information could circulate out in the world. After a while, it became a sort of unspoken rule that you just didn't mess with the library. You can't fight there. You just don't. And you don't steal from the library, either.

So that's the library. I know there's another functional one in the state somewhere, which is neat. Maybe we'll have a place to put any extra copies of books. Spread the love, y'know?

That's what I love about the place. They don't hoard anything, and nothing's sacred, which I know seems counterintuitive. But what good is knowledge if people can't get to it? Otherwise it just sits there gathering dust.

Last time I went, I told Norman—he's the chief librarian—about my plan to get the radio station running again, and he just laughed. Crotchety old fart. I respect what he does, but that doesn't mean he's a nice guy. East-Coaster. I dunno what that means, but that's what Doctor Judee calls him. She and her sister are from New York, and they make sure everyone knows it.

So anyway, Theo will take over the walkie-talkie situation while I run errands in Roslyn. Hoping to find something on transistor radios. Been thinking about fixing up small radios, too, just for tuning in. Not that radio's broadcasting anymore, but still. Maybe one of these days I can play some music over the frequency, and the guys sitting up on the walls can tune in.

Best to get the tower up before the rains come. Biters love the rain.

[Click]

6: BRIDE

It rained all night.

Rafael was gone by the time Jo shuffled out of her room. She dressed in the dark and eyed the cabin windows. Biters loved the rain.

Jo met Nell on the outskirts of the concrete town. They spread their coats over their heads like tents and sprinted towards the HQ building. Jo felt mud squelching through the soles of her boots and wondered if Rafael could look out for a new pair when he went out again.

"Ruben. Tom," Rafael barked. Two Wolfskins with sour faces nodded. "Trees are creeping back toward the walls. Can't have that if we want to keep the biters off us. Take a few recruits and trim it back."

He turned. "Sienna."

His second-in-command lifted her chin in lazy acknowledgment. She was thin, all angles and wild red hair, but Jo had watched her fire a heavy shotgun without flinching.

"Lookouts spotted a small group of biters moving up the hill," Rafael said. "Ten miles out."

Sienna smiled, crooked.

"Want me to try your little trick?" she asked. "What do you call it? Shepherding. Like they're goats?"

Rafael didn't smile.

"Do what you want," he said. "But take one or two people with you."

Sienna's pale eyes slid to Nell.

"She'll do," she said. "Good practice to get up close with the biters."

"It's dangerous out there for apprentices," he said.

"She's Wolfskin-bound," Sienna shot back. "Nell can handle it."

Nell straightened. Sienna didn't argue for people she didn't intend to back.

Rafael's gaze shifted.

"Then take the other apprentice, too."

Jo's stomach dropped.

Sienna grimaced and looked for a moment as though she was going to bite back with something. The moment passed.

"Fine," she said. "C'mon, girlies." She brushed past them and snatched the stable keys from the hook. "Let's see how the biters feel about company."

Rafael bent to give Jo a quick word.

"Be careful," he said. "Like we practiced. The herding doesn't always work. Biters need to be in a kind of mood to be moved around. Still." A beat. "Keep your gun close."

Her heart was beating considerably faster now. She and Nell followed Sienna to gear up. They loaded a small pistol each, a hunting knife, and a handheld noisemaker.

Rafael had built the devices months ago, after Jo found the noisy gray box. It had given him the idea that perhaps, biters could be persuaded with noise. Sound could pull biters. Maybe, if handled right, it could also push them. He'd pointed to old hunting tricks, machines that copied prey calls, anything loud enough to draw attention and simple enough to guide it.

Jo had shepherded before, just not with biters.

She pulled her hood over her beanie, shivering with cold and anticipation. Nell mirrored her, flashing a quick, eager look as they swung up onto the horses.

Their mounts pawed the muddy ground, and Sienna led the way out the gates, off the main path, and through the woods. Rain tapped against Jo's knuckles as she tightened her grip on the reins. The rhythm of the horse's hooves carried up through her legs and into her chest, forcing her to breathe with it. The farther they rode, the quieter the woods became.

"How much further?" Nell called, her voice betraying a squeak over the wind. Sienna didn't answer, and Nell didn't ask again.

When they came to a clearing where the only noise was rain pattering on the branches, Sienna pulled her horse to a stop.

"You do what we practiced," she said to Nell. Nell nodded obediently.

Sienna's attention snapped to Jo.

"You think you can follow directions, princess?" she asked. "Without your daddy around?"

Heat rushed to Jo's face. She should have known that was coming. She squared her shoulders and nodded once.

"We'll see."

Movement crested the hill ahead of them. At first it looked like people, a loose crowd of heads bobbing into view. Then the shapes resolved, broken and wrapped in rot. The biters were slow with cold, but they were moving and that was enough.

"You two take the left," Sienna said. "I'll take the right.

Two arm-lengths apart. Use the crops first. Once they lock on, hit the buzzers."

She glanced between them.

"We lead them down the slope, so stay together. And don't get bit." She kicked her horse and took off like a bullet.

"You, um, want the middle?" Nell asked. Her eyes stayed on the advancing mass. Her horse danced. Jo nodded and pressed her heels into her mount.

The biters moved closer in a smear of muted greens and slate, flashes of yellow threading through their bodies.

Sienna hit the buzzer.

The sound tore through the rain and the biters' heads jerked in unison. The horde stalled, then bent sideways toward her.

Nell cracked her riding crop. The nearest biters flinched and leaned away, their feet scraping as they corrected.

Jo pushed her horse forward before she could think better of it. She triggered her buzzer. The biters closest to her faltered, pulled toward the noise.

She shifted left, keeping space between them. Buzzed again.

They drifted after her, uneven and sluggish. She kept riding, watching hands and mouths, ready to bolt if one lunged.

Sienna turned downhill. The horde sagged with her, bodies following the slope like mud.

Jo's chest loosened. She tracked the distance as they moved away, watched the yellow growth crawling over their backs.

Distance was good. A real bite was what carried the parasite. As long as she kept space—a scream tore through the clearing.

Jo spun. To her right, Nell was down, flat on her back. A biter twice her size loomed over her, one dead hand locked around Nell's boot. Moss filled the gaps where flesh had sloughed away, vines knotted through bone and tendon.

"Help!" Nell screamed, kicking. "Help me!"

Jo vaulted off her horse and hit the ground wrong. Mud slid under her boots and she went down hard. The biter lunged.

Its hand caught her jacket and yanked. Jo slammed into the mud, breath knocked loose. Its face dropped toward hers, teeth clicking, breath thick and rotten.

Knife.

Her hands were braced against its chest, keeping the weight off her throat. The thing jerked and thrashed and fought to close the gap.

"Move!"

Instinct intact, Jo ducked.

Gunfire cracked over her head. Three shots, close and loud. The biter's grip went slack. It sagged, then collapsed, brown liquid bubbling out of its skull as it folded into the ground with a low, wet sound.

Nell was talking, but all Jo could hear was a ringing in her ears.

"…didn't even notice it grabbed me!" Nell said, words rushing now. "You *saw* it and you just *stood* there, Jo! With that dumb look on your–"

Sienna seized Nell by the collar and hauled her upright.

"You get bit?"

"No. Ow, just twisted my ankle. I don't think–"

Sienna didn't wait. She ran her hands over Nell's legs, her arms, her neck, checking skin and seams. Only then did she let go.

Sienna's eyes went to Jo.

Jo lay in the grass, hands still up, fingers shaking. The buzzer was gone. Sienna must have tossed it down the slope with the rest of the noise.

Sienna stepped closer and pressed the gun barrel into Jo's cheek.

"What about you?" she asked cooly.

Jo shook her head.

"Show me." The gun *clicked.*

Jo's hands were shaking so much that it took her three tries to unzip her coat and roll up her sleeves. Her skin was dark and scarred, but unbroken.

Sienna didn't blink.

"Nell."

Nell came into view and crouched beside her, without meeting her eyes. Her hands checked ribs, arms, legs, and the back of her jacket.

"Not bit," Nell declared after a tense silence. Sienna lowered the gun, but not all the way.

"You were supposed to stay together," she snarled. "You were supposed to watch her. Your partner went down and you didn't stop it. What do you have to say?"

Jo opened her mouth, closed it, and knew there wasn't anything coming out this time

Sienna snorted.

"Can't believe I got stuck with the mute," she said. "Comes and goes, does it?

"Convenient."

Jo stared at the grass. Her jaw locked and refused to open again. Sienna turned away.

"Get up," she said. "We're done here."

"You're gonna be a Wolfskin," Rafael said that evening, bursting into the cabin with his arms wide. "Official meeting's next week. That sink in yet?"

Jo shot him a look and went back to the sewing kit.

"Hey," Rafael said, dragging a chair closer. "Don't do that." He watched her hands. "This about today?"

Jo pulled a length of fishing wire free. She braced her torn boot on her knee and threaded the needle without looking up.

"Sienna says what she wants," Rafael went on. "She's backing Nell, of course she is. That's her apprentice." He leaned forward. "But it's not her call."

Jo tugged the wire tight.

"It's mine too," he said. "And I'm telling you, you're getting in."

"I'm not," Jo said.

"I know you can do it," Rafael went on. "Your instincts are good, and you're the best shot I've trained." He smiled, beard lifting. "I just need to lock it in with the council and the General and—"

"I can't." Jo yanked the wire too hard. It bit into the callous on her finger.

"Don't say that."

"I almost got Nell k-killed."

"She's loud. You'd have survived her either way," Rafael said. Then, quicker, "Joking."

Jo searched for the right words and came up short.

"Wolfskins don't have…m-malfunctions."

Rafael waved a hand.

"Please. Half the team's a malfunction." He snorted. "Remember Ruben leaving the stable doors open? Lost a quarter of the mounts."

Jo bent over her boot, pushing the needle through the soft leather. She didn't look up. "And if you're a Wolfskin," Rafael said, "you're untouchable."

"Not to Hayes."

The needle slid free. Jo felt Rafael watching her.

After a moment, he said it slower.

"Hayes can't touch you." A pause. "You're not one of his brides anymore. You're my daughter. His rules say that counts, even against him."

Jo wrapped the twine around her finger, tight enough to feel her pulse.

"You're gonna be good," Rafael said. "Better than good." His eyes sharpened, fire returning to them. "You'll raise hell. And no one's gonna lay a hand on you again."

Jo fixed her watery gaze on the floorboards.

"You don't gotta talk," Rafael added.

She was relieved for that.

Jo came with nothing this time. Her pack was empty and she had no trinkets to offer. She knew Snow would notice.

Still, that afternoon, her feet carried her toward the concrete tower. Frost glazed the ground in a thin skin, brittle underfoot. She followed the fence, stepping where the dirt showed through, until she reached the bent bars and slipped through. She crouched by the wall, breath held, and checked the balcony above. For a lookout, or the General.

The courtyard lay quiet.

Jo stayed low and waited, legs burning as time stretched. She usually heard their voices by now, chattering lightly, usually as a signal that Jo was safe to come out. But nothing stirred, not even a bird.

She waited longer, watching the shadows slide away from her boots. When the stillness pressed too hard, she moved again, creeping along the fence toward the tower and keeping to the dark.

She finally found Faith, sitting alone on the low bench by the cool wall, hands folded tight in her lap.

She looked up when Jo drew close. Her eyes were red and dry.

"You shouldn't be here," she said, in a voice stern and sad.

Jo glanced past her, down the path, then back.

Faith followed her look.

"Snow's not coming today," she said. Jo stood there, hands loose at her sides.

"D-did—"

"They found her things," Faith said. Her delicate fingers twisted in the fabric of her skirt. "She didn't hide them well enough."

Jo sucked in a breath.

Snow never got caught, she was too careful. She was meticulous in how she told Jo exactly what to look for when she went out. *Get this kind of metal, it should do this when you hold it up to the light. You have to find the watch with this kind of insignia, I already have that one.* Jo used to repeat Snow's instructions to herself while she walked, over and over, so she wouldn't forget. There was no paper for lists, or any other way to mark it down.

"W-where d-did they take her?" Jo demanded. She scanned the courtyard, the base of the tower, the doors, the patch of dirt near the wall where it was soft. She'd dig if she had to. She'd tear the place apart.

"We don't know," Faith said.

Jo swallowed. "M-maybe someone r-redeemed her. L-like you said. Maybe–"

"No," Faith said. The word came fast. "He was angry. More than I've ever seen him." Her hand brushed her belly. "They don't do that anymore."

The image of Snow outside the walls sent a cold chill through Jo's chest. She thought of Ruth's eyes, gone, only dark hollows left behind. Her stomach rolled.

Faith watched her, tears held in place by sheer force.

"You can't come back, Johanna," she whispered urgently. "Not tomorrow, not ever again. You don't belong to this place anymore, and that's the only thing keeping you alive."

Jo started to protest, unable to get the word out. No, she thought, working her jaw. No.

But Faith stood up and practically shoved Jo back towards the fence.

"Go now," she hissed. "Before the guard comes."

Jo backed away. Her heel scraped the stone, too loud. Faith had turned away, hand clamped over her eyes, and Jo slipped through the fence; she didn't stop moving until the tower was well behind her.

Dinner was served in the mess hall, but the sky was clear, so Jo took her bowl outside and ate by the fires.

People grumbled over the small portions and Jo savored every moment spent close to the heat. As she ate slowly, to prolong the feeling of eating the beans and bits of jerky, she listened to the light conversations floating around the square.

There was the usual talk of biter sightings and when they expected the next trade to happen. *More biters by the gates? They're getting more ballsy every year. Well, the frost was melting so that made sense.*

Jo only backed up from the campfire when her coat started to smoke. With her bowl empty, she scanned the circle of light. Faces flickered in and out of view. Nell usually found her for meals and they sat together, but she wasn't there.

Come to think of it, Jo hadn't seen her at all since the herding. Standing alone by the fire made her feel exposed. She moved to a log at the edge of the square and sat. Cold soaked through her pants.

"…swear if I gotta eat this tripe one more time I'm gonna tear someone up."

Ruben's voice cut through the low talk. One of Rafael's Wolfskins. He even looked the part, jaw jutting, skin pulled tight and sallow.

"There ain't any meat left," someone said. "You think the biters are eating all the deer?"

"They don't eat," someone said. "They get sunlight."

"Tell that to anyone they've bitten."

A few laughs.

Ruben licked his bowl clean and dropped it in the dirt.

"Parasites move on when they find something better," he said, eyes on Tom. "Like when your wife got tired of you and hopped to one of the General's beds."

"She was chosen," Tom muttered. "It was an honor."

Ruben's beady eyes went to Jo. She dropped her gaze into the flames until her eyes burned. She should've gone home instead of waiting for Nell.

"I hear there's talk of another trade," said Liam, one of the younger recruits. His boyish face looked eager in the flickering flames. "With Kettering."

"A trade," someone said, "or something else?"

Jo stilled.

"B-but we've g-got a truce," she said. The words came out before she could stop them.

Liam looked surprised to hear her speak. He shrugged. "We've been hunting on their land." Ruben spread his fingers in the dirt like he was mapping something out. "They're right by a river too. We'd have better access to water. We set up another Burning Well and—"

"That's enough."

The talk died as Rafael stepped into the firelight.

"I'd quit speculating about things you don't understand," he said.

"No offense, Raf," Ruben said, "but you got made Captain fast. Can't blame you for not knowing how things really run."

Rafael's jaw tightened.

"It's Captain to you," he said. "Our truce with Kettering stands. Anyone who says otherwise can join Cecil on the pyre."

The Wolfskins went quiet and bent over their bowls.

Jo thought she saw Ruben's eyes flash but it could have been a trick of the flames.

Jo reported for duty at first light.

The wall was rimed with frost. It cracked under her boots if she stepped wrong, so she kept to the worn patches where others had paced before her. Below, the slope fell away into gray trees and rock.

She dragged her glove along the concrete and felt the raised bump of old graffiti under the paint, buried now beneath layers of white. She couldn't make out the words anymore, which felt like a waste. Even something crude would've broken up all the gray.

Rafael hadn't come home after dinner the night before. His chair had been empty when she woke.

When the council met like this, they didn't break until they were done with you. Jo rested her rifle on her knees and watched her breath fog and fade. A pair of Wolfskins passed below her spot on the wall. She caught a few words as they went.

"—Sienna's training her now."

"About time."

Nell should've been up here with her. Instead, Jo pictured the training yard. Sienna's red hair bouncing around as she paced and barked at Nell's ready-stance. Sienna had been pulling Nell from wall duty more and more lately. Wolfskins didn't stand around waiting for something to happen.

After the herding, Jo didn't expect to be pulled anywhere. If she wasn't becoming a Wolfskin, then this was it.

She scanned the treeline, then felt stupid for it, like Snow might wander back in from the trees if Jo watched long enough.

Then, a horn sounded somewhere inside the walls.

Below, figures hurried towards the square, coming out of every building Jo could see. They left their tools on the ground.

Sienna crossed the yard with purpose, Ruben at her side. Nell followed a step behind them, still limping from the herding incident. Ruben didn't usually bother with training recruits, not unless he'd already made up his mind.

A runner waved her down from the wall, but Jo didn't move right away. Up there, the ground was far.She stayed until the runner called again, sharper this time.

Jo climbed down, boots stiff on the rungs, and hit the yard hard. She kept her eyes off Rafael as she joined the others in front of the council building, already bracing for the words she didn't want to hear.

The white doors opened.

A man stepped out into the sun, his shape cutting it in half. His heavy coat was draped over his angled shoulders and the collection of gold, silver, and red bars set on his military jacket glimmered like eyes in the dark. A hush rippled over the workers as they hoped he wouldn't look their way.

"Go on, Captain," the General said, hands clasped behind his back.

Rafael stepped forward, and found Jo in the crowd. His mouth twitched, proud and tight at the corners. Somehow the image of him standing in tandem with the General felt like a betrayal.

"The council has reached a decision," Rafael said, voice carrying. "For the coming mission to Kettering, the Wolfskins will take two apprentices."

A ripple moved through the crowd. That didn't happen.

Rafael went on.

"Both will be evaluated in the field. Afterward, a final decision will be made."

Nell's face went pale. She looked at Jo, then away, like she wasn't sure which direction she was allowed to face.

Sienna's face remained impassive. Whatever she thought, she didn't say it.

General Hayes's gaze slid across the square and stopped on Jo, and he bared his teeth in what she feared was a smile. The heat of it pinned her in place.

She always told herself that she was free of him, but the way her body betrayed her in that moment made her feel bound and as silent as she was when she was a bride.

7: WORKING TITLE

RADIO LOG 04
"Working Title"
Location: Ambridge

[A click]

A BOISTEROUS VOICE (humming a jaunty tune): Bum-ba-da bada-badaaaaaa… Aaaaand we're back!

Thank you for tuning into The Show That We Actually Can't Broadcast Live So We Just Record It. That's a working title, by the way. I'm your host, Prophet, and with me here tonight is Fisher. Say hello, Fisher!

FISHER: Hello. And can I say, as much as I think the code names are wacky and silly and on-brand, I don't see the point in using them, Ez. Is someone going to be listening to this besides you?

PROPHET: Maybe someday! That would be the dream. And anyway, I wanna practice.

FISHER: In that case, can I be "Gilmore"? There's a ring to that. Or "Kirk." Kirk's a good guy, even though he annoyed me at first, but I think he grew on us all.

PROPHET: Because you're my brother, I'm gonna let you be whatever stupid character you wanna be. But I do want to offer a warning that branding yourself as a "Gilmore Girls" fan could stick, and you should just be prepared for that.

I think this is a good time to clarify for our audience that Fisher—sorry, Gilmore? Is that really what we're going with?—is now a proud owner of the highly sought-after video cassette box set of *Gilmore Girls*.

GILMORE: All I need is season six to complete the set.

PROPHET: For anyone listening and as confused as I used to be, back during the Television Times everyone watched a new episode of their

show every week. *Gilmore Girls,* from what I understand, is one from the year 2000-ish.
Everyone in the show lives in this town where it's always Fall, and they carry around these papery cups with no liquid in them, and they're always, always, always talking.

GILMORE: You're always, always, always–

PROPHET: Hey, wait sec–

GILMORE: Now you know how it feels then, don't you? To be on the receiving end of that constant stream of–

PROPHET: Yeah, so, these Gilmore girls walk around and talk, and they have problems I guess, but they're low-stakes. It's stuff like, "Oh no, my rich mother wants to pay for my daughter's school, but she'll only give me the money if I come to dinner. Oh nooooo." I didn't know you had to pay to get educated.

GILMORE: Different monsters, man.

PROPHET: You've seen everything but the sixth season, you said?

GILMORE: Yeah, season five leaves you on this horrible cliffhanger. I need to see what happens to Rory after Lorelai catches her sleeping with her ex. He's married, Prophet. Married. Honestly, I was shocked at how out of character that was, but seeing the seasons that come after, it's all downhill from there.

PROPHET: Do we need to make today's broadcast about the show you've been religiously watching on loop for the past ten years?

GILMORE: I would like to request a segment on the show, yes. And, plus, that's Old-World Media, right? Boom. That's part of our entertainment section.

PROPHET: So an Apocalypse Train lineup would look something like: News and Updates, Safety Reminders, Obituaries, and…*Gilmore Girls,* where all we discuss is *Gilmore Girls?*

GILMORE: Just Gilmore Girls, yes.

[A pause]

[Scribbling]

PROPHET: Fine, we'll throw it in.

GILMORE: Awesome.

PROPHET: I guess it's time for me to see what all the fuss is about, anyway.

GILMORE: Wait…really? You'll sit and watch with me? You do know what you're committing to, right?

PROPHET: I think I need to understand why you love it so much, and this is the first step to unraveling the mystery that enshrouds my brother.

GILMORE: Oh, I hate it.

PROPHET: You…but you said——

GILMORE: And I love it.

PROPHET: I don't——

GILMORE: It's a love-hate relationship. You'll see.
PROPHET: Sounds toxic.
GILMORE: Toxic, yes. Stakes? Low. Vibes? Cozy. It's a nice little escape, to see how the world was before.

[A chair creaks]

PROPHET: Aaaaaand that's a beautiful transition to why we want to make this broadcast real, to talk live, to send our little conversations over the sound waves right to your radio. The goal of this little broadcast is to bring a little news, a little fun, a way to connect with our sister communities—

GILMORE: —once we make the technology available—

PROPHET: —and bring a little light into these dark nights.
GILMORE: And Apocalypse Train.

PROPHET: Yes.

GILMORE: That's the title we're going with?

PROPHET: Like a train of thought.

GILMORE: Ah.

PROPHET: You no like?

GILMORE: No, I like.

PROPHET: We can change it.

GILMORE: Hey, I'm all aboard. Choo-choo. Just…do you think "apocalypse" is too…how do you say…?

PROPHET: Bleak?

GILMORE: Is it too on-the-nose? It was funny calling life the apocalypse as a joke, like ha-ha, look how bad it's gotten. But now that it's…real and we're in it…

PROPHET: No, I hear you. That's a good note. It's workshopable . What about…Paradise Found?

GILMORE: Hm. I like that less.

PROPHET: A funny little play on an existing book title, and a play on words.

GILMORE: Um, yeah, no.

PROPHET: Well, c'mon. Give me yours. You can add a sprinkle of your very favorite show.

GILMORE: Ooh, don't give me that power, brother.
PROPHET: C'mon. Give it to me.
GILMORE: Okay, well, Rory ends up working for the Yale Daily News—Yale's a college, by the way—

PROPHET: I may not have been to a college but I know what one is.

GILMORE: But Rory's not my favorite. Maybe a play on Luke's Diner, which is where they always go to eat and drink their coffee and then go to work or school.

PROPHET: We don't have work or school.

GILMORE: It's like the transitory space. I dunno. I'm spitballing.

PROPHET: Spitball away. When we come back, we just might have a title. Or several.

GILMORE: Stay tuned, Ambridge.

PROPHET: Be safe out there, and goodnight! [A click]

8: STRANGERS

RADIO LOG 05
Location: Ambridge

EZRA: Okay, how is it that the perfect siblings Ruth and Judee can get approved for a generator, but me and Theo can't? They don't even need one. All they do is surgeries and stuff. This whole experiment is just exchanging problems for bigger problems.

Plus, I'm not super keen on venturing outside of Ambridge to find one at the moment. It's getting a little weird out there, and not the normal kind of weird we're used to.

So when I was in Roslyn reading the books, trading our crap for their crap, standard procedure stuff, Norm told me that right before I came along, a group of strangers knocked on Roslyn's gate. It's not often Roslyn gets visitors except Ambridge and Suncrest, our other sister towns. These guys called themselves "Burning Well."

And let me tell you, these guys were stocked. They traded some really nice weapons—military-grade, great for offing biters quickly—some MRE rations, and big warm coats. I don't know why they'd risk approaching towns they don't even know bearing all these good gifts. Norm thought they might be US military, but I don't know. I thought the government went to pieces years ago.

So Burning Well said they were looking for trainable soldiers and workers to "come and be a part of the new thing." They claimed that Burning Well was impenetrable to biters, had the best training around, and that by preserving the human race, we could "create a new one to fill the world."

Okay, the way I say that sounds really culty. I guess when I step back it's like, yeah, I get it. So many of us have been wiped out while the biters take over everything like the big, stupid, evil weeds they are. Burning Well seems like they're doing something about it.

But it gets a little weirder.

They really seemed interested in asking about, uh, Roslyn's fertility rate? I guess there's really only one logical way to repopulate the earth.

Eugh. Yeah. Still. I dunno. Norm didn't look happy at all about that bit.

He told Burning Well that Roslyn would consider the offer for whoever wanted to join. Honestly, I think he just said it to get those creeps out of there.

[Click]

9: CLOSE CALLS & PRIORITIES

RADIO LOG 06
Location: Ambridge

EZRA: The rains are here, and they're bad. The kind of bad that throws a huge monkey wrench into my plans of getting the walkies working. I haven't had a second to look over the notes I got from Roslyn, because Birdie has all of us working around the clock on weed duty, and not the fun kind of weed, I might add.

Since the biters out there are part plant, part Ent if you're a Tolkien reader, part alien probably, it's pretty much all hands on deck when it rains.

The biters usually don't give us much trouble in the winter since they're all cold and stiff, but in the spring they start getting big and fat and fast.

Which makes me wonder, why are they so obsessed with bothering us when they seem to be well-fed already?

I think Ruth tried to explain to me once that because they're parasitic in nature, they automatically look for something alive that they can…implant the next generation of seeds? Something sick like that. Not something I like thinking about extensively.

Since biters love being around growth, me and Theo have been hacking at every green thing in sight besides what's in the greenhouse, but we come back a day later and everything's sprung up again. And we have to be extra careful not to step on anything. There've been a couple of close calls, so Birdie's been making us wear shoulder-high gloves and the big, rubber fishing pants when we go out in the grass. They're pretty horrible to move around in, but at least nothing can bite through.

We did have some biters breach the south fence the other day. Kind of a close call, to be honest. The rain has just been making everything all rotted, and we hadn't had time to take a look at the weak points in the fence when we're already busting our asses just keeping the biters off of us. Theo actually had one clamped on his ankle for a minute before I weed-hacked it off. He wasn't bit. Judee made sure to check him like, twenty times.

Again, we gotta thank Birdie for making us wear those heinous boots. Still scary though. They move way faster when it rains. *Yich.*

I think it's gonna be a minute before I can visit the radio station again. Priorities and all that.

[Click]

10: GREEN LIGHT

RADIO LOG 07
Location: Ambridge

EZRA: Birdie *liked* it. She liked our silly little pretend radio show. And do you know the weirdest thing? I cannot make this up. Keeping the *Gilmore Girls* crap ended up being our edge because apparently, Birdie used to be obsessed with the show. Like, she was the person who memorized entire episodes when they aired back then.

She and Theo talked for a straight thirty minutes while I stood there ready to defend my case, and show her the charts I made, but ultimately, they didn't need me at all. Truth and *Gilmore Girls* prevailed.

That's a sentence I never thought I'd say.

The radio show is a passion project, and it would require a whole lot more range to actually broadcast something out into the world. But I guess it worked to get Birdie on board. She's much more keen to help us out since I guess she and Theo are best friends now, which is great for me. I need investors in the dream. She's going to put some more people on our team.

Oh, and I guess that brings me to my next point. It's not a big deal, but I thought you might want to know: the walkie-talkies are finally, *finally*, working.

They're working. They're actually working! I could sing. I won't, to spare your ears, but just know I'm beside myself.

A team. For the comms tower. It's going to be a thing. We've got our scouts, our runners, our snipers, animal handlers, and gardeners, and medics, but now…

…we've got communications.

[Click]

11: DEPART

"What's Kettering like?"

Rafael folded a pair of thick socks and pressed them flat.

"Old hospital," he said. "Huge campus, all sectioned off. It's past time for a trade." He continued to pack his bag: buzzers, an empty water bottle, some rations, and an extra hunting knife even though he kept a few on his person. "They've got real medicine, and food. Better greenhouse than us. And generators. And chickens."

Jo unpacked her bag again, counted her thermal shirts, and set to re-folding them. "What will we h-have to d-do?"

"Stick with the team. Keep the biters off while the trade happens." Rafael shrugged. "Simple enough."
"You and Nell'll be fine. Once they see what you can do—"

Jo rolled a shirt tight and wedged it into the corner of her bag.

"Raf," she said. The word caught. She cleared her throat. "W-what if I don't?"

"Don't what, kiddo," Rafael hummed.

She stared at the zipper.

"Fit," she said finally.

He stared at her, a pause loosening his jaw. After a tense moment, his smile returned, too bright.

"Funny," he said and shoved another pair of socks into his pack. "Don't let Sienna scare you. She's all bark and no bite."
"S'not her," Jo mumbled.
"What, then?"

Jo wished she could articulate what she felt that afternoon: the cold shock of dread she got when Hayes appeared like a shadow, or when he looked down at her. She sometimes forgot she lived in the same city, since Rafael kept her far from his house. But his hands stretched along the whole city, paralyzing her.

"I don't want to be…close," she said. The word felt safer than the rest. "N-not to him."
Rafael's hands stilled on a pack of crackers.

"The Wolfskins don't serve the General," he said, slow and careful. "We serve the city. And what makes you think you'll have to ever go near him?" He frowned. "You're not makin' sense, Jo."

Jo shoved another shirt into her bag harder than she meant to.
"F-forget it," she said. "Shouldn't have said anything."
Rafael exhaled through his nose.

"The Wolfskins give you room to move. You telling me you wanna shovel shit for the rest of your life?"

"I don't wanna *be* here for the rest of my life."

She could feel Rafael's eyes on her back.

"You've seen what's outside the walls," he said finally. "All those biters. They were people once, you know. People with nowhere to go."

He tapped the crackers into place.

"Burning Well's the safest place there is, and I've been out there more times than you can count."

Jo zipped her bag and sat on it to force it closed. Rafael followed Jo to the kitchen nook where she grabbed an insulation bag and shoved packs of rations into it.

"C'mon, Jo," he said. "Don't shut down again. Talk to me."

"I s-served h-him for years," she said between her teeth. "I don't want to ever…s-see h-him a-ag-g—"

Two big, solid hands landed on her shoulders. She bit the inside of her cheek, afraid she might let out a sob. She felt like a child.

Rafae turned her to face him, his expression set.

"The General's got his way of doing things in his house," he said. "I don't agree with it. And I can't imagine what you went through."

He hesitated, then went on, voice lower.

"Sometimes I hate the bastard for it."

Jo blinked. Rafael had never, ever spoken that way against the General.

"But you don't belong to Hayes anymore," Rafael said. "And you gotta start acting like it. I know living here ain't ideal and it don't feel good sometimes. But if I ever found you dead-walking out there…"

Rafael cleared his throat and it seemed to take him a moment to steady his voice.

"At least we got rules in here. There's order. And ranks. We can work with that. And we got each other, don't we?"

The fight went out of her. She leaned into him without thinking, forehead pressing into his chest. He held her there until her breathing evened out.

The morning of the Wolfskins' departure dawned with the promise of rain. It was hard to tell if the sun was up at all. From her window, Jo could just make out the route west—a narrow path that slipped into a stand of firs and vanished.

Rafael had already left, but Jo was glad for the chance to approach the others of her own accord. She sat facing west for a minute and dragged a finger along the windowsill, following a split in the wood she knew by heart.

Anticipation coursed hot through Jo's chest as she donned her layers to brave the cold: wool, canvas, her freshly-sewn boots. As she went for her knapsack, she noticed the side table was bare. The radio was gone.

She stood there a second, looking at the empty space. It wouldn't make sense for Rafael to take it. He wouldn't take up precious space with something relatively useless. Still, she couldn't be sure.

Jo went to the far wall and knelt by the broken vent, where she kept what little she'd found worth saving. She pried the panel loose and pushed aside bent watches and a velvet box of soot-darkened gold teeth. The map was tucked inside an old cigarette case, folded tight. She unrolled it across her knee.

The center square was the wall, she knew that much. To the right, the campground, the place where she'd found the biter. Ruth. She traced the line with her thumb. On the back, faint and water-stained, were marks so small she'd missed them at first. A dip in the path and a cluster of scratches. Trees, maybe. There was a dip to signal a valley. She'd never gone that far past the mountain.

At night, she used to study it by candlelight, smoothing the creases, tracing the lines until her eyes watered and her fingers stained with ink. She'd wondered who drew it, or what they were planning. She thought of Ruth, of the radio in the dirt near her, and felt the familiar slide of questions crop up with nowhere to land.

There wasn't time for them now.

Jo folded the map once and slipped it into the narrow pocket she'd sewn into the lining of her boot.

She shut the vent and took one last look at the cramped quarters of the cabin, of the tattered wall hangings and familiar stacks of cups, of her wool comforter and Rafael's workbench. She burned the image into her memory, and stepped outside.

On her way to the gates, Jo slowed at the General's courtyard.

There was no one on the path today. It was beginning to rain. Jo stopped at the broken fence and looked up at the balcony far above the ground, then at the place Snow used to pass by. Jo looked, but remembering Faith's warning, didn't go a step further.

The Wolfskins assembled at the front gate. Everyone seemed too preoccupied with their mounts to notice Jo's arrival, which was just as well. Jo wove through the small crowd of disgruntled hunters towards the stable doors where she was handed the reins of a small bay. The old horse allowed Jo to saddle him. He blew warm air in her face, which was welcome because the temperature in the barn dropped when Nell walked in.

She breezed past Jo and saddled her mount.

"Nell," said Jo. The word sounded like it had run through gravel. Nell continued tugging on the girth.

Jo tried again.

"Got to k-keep your hair long?"

Nell glanced at her long braid, fingers tightening around it.

"Yeah," she said. "For a little longer, anyway."

Nell favored one foot when she crossed the stall. She paused to steady herself before reaching for the bridle.

"Didn't think they'd send us both," she said.

She didn't say anything else, and Jo let it be. They'd have a few days on the road together and quiet was better than pressing.

Theirs was a team of fourteen including Nell and Jo: mostly men plus Sienna and Barb. It had been months since the entire team was assembled. Jo could only guess that they were all eager to taste the valley air, and perhaps get first dibs on supplies. The perks of being a Wolfskin.

"Headin' out!" barked Sienna and everyone swung into their saddles.

She and her stallion danced in front of the company behind a stoic Rafael. He nodded once to Jo—they'd agreed that he'd treat her like any other soldier—and then to the guards manning the gate. The doors groaned open.

Jo craned around to give the city one last look. Smoke thinned in the morning air. The wall rose pale and unbroken, except for one dark shape near the top.

A man stood there, still as a marker. The metal on his jacket caught the new light when he moved, a brief flash before he settled again. Watching.

Jo adjusted her reins and faced forward. Rafael had said ranks mattered, that order kept people safe. She held on to that as the horses started down the road, even as the image of Snow pressed at the back of her mind.

When Jo glanced back again, the silhouette was already gone, swallowed by the concrete as the gates closed behind them.

They were not far from the forest, and the stench of petrichor filled Jo's nostrils. Winter was quickly dying, and the scent of rain lingered like a carcass in the sun. As they descended the mountain, the trees thickened, and Jo could see people reaching for their weapons. She brushed her fingers against the knife handle at her hip.

Fortunately, the party didn't see any biters until they were well past the stream. It seemed that the hunters had been doing a fair job keeping them at bay. The line of horses clopped past the old crossroads sign, which was too weather-beaten to read, and that was when they heard a rustling in the thicket followed by the telltale throaty noise.

"Ruben," said Rafael.

The caravan kept a slow pace as Ruben hopped off his horse and trudged towards the sound, machete gleaming against the stony green. Like most of the Wolfskins, Ruben was a walking wall of muscle. His shoulders jutted out, and strength rippled where he gripped his weapon. He raised his blade and the biter's hiss was silenced.

They passed a handful of biters in the trees. Jo clocked them first as flowers, pale and low to the ground, until one of them moved. An arm slid forward, skin torn wide where roots threaded through muscle, dull yellow against gray flesh.

The air became slightly sweeter after a day's ride from Burning Well. Jo was relieved to leave the forest behind and everything growing in it. They trod along packed dirt paths with rolling hills, and the party was in good humor. They stopped only when it was too dark to see and made camp at the base of a small cliffside.

Jo could kill a biter without getting a scratch, she was taught to hunt and use every part of the animal afterwards, and she could navigate with the stars and the moss on the trees. What she couldn't do easily was fit into a group. But she would have to try, for Rafael's sake at least.

The group stayed up late, swapping jokes and getting rowdy. Nell was sandwiched between Sienna and Ruben, cackling at something he'd said. Jo tried her best to look interested in the conversation on her end of the fire, but ultimately wished for a moment where she could prove herself in a non-verbal setting. She vaguely wondered if anyone would be impressed with how little time it took her to skin a deer, and decided not.

The next evening, they passed the river. Rafael called for an early camp to water the horses and refill their water containers, so Jo led her bay to the stream, and he drank in slurping gulps. She had to pull his head back a few times to keep him from choking. He was old; his hooves were cracked from age and trudging on wet roads. Jo scratched his matted head.

She was relieved when Rafael sent her to gather firewood— something to do—so Jo left her steed and trumped into the woods, yanking her thick socks over her pant legs to prevent anything unwanted from slithering up there. Most of the fallen branches were damp with the recent snow so she trekked along the dirt path to dryer ground.

The light was fading fast and it was getting harder to see where she was stepping. Footsteps through the underbrush came closer and, in a moment, Ruben appeared. He stood as still as one of the bare trees and watched her work. His face caught a gleam of setting sunlight and it turned his cheeks hollow.

When Ruben spoke his voice was soft with a lilt that was almost playful.

"Jo," he said, mouth curling around her name. "You ain't gonna make friends if you're always off by your lonesome."

She shifted her armful of sticks and tried to seem unbothered.

"You're gonna have to speak up, girl," Ruben chuckled and ventured a step closer. "Let me help you with your sticks. If you're gonna be on our team, you gotta let other people help you, dontcha think?"

Jo felt ice creep into her fingers and gripped a stick so hard it punctured her palm. Out in the woods, there were no locks, no doors, no Rafael, and nothing but her hunting knife to protect her when a man came too close.

"But you only got recruited because of your daddy. Everybody knows that," Ruben continued, stepping again so a twig snapped.

She slid her hand to her belt and curled her hand around her knife.

"Can't see how much help you'd be with vocal chords that don't work very well, huh? Do they still work, or are you just messing with all of us? Pretending you got that cute little stutter?" He leaned in. His breath smelled like dead things. "Can you still scream?"

Jo's pulse snapped in her throat and she tripped in the opposite direction back to camp, as Ruben chuckled behind her.

She stayed in the light of the campfire and sat on her hands so no one would notice them shaking. The company chatted and chewed their jerky. Her new awareness made her watch them all with suspicion.

Ruben crashed through the brush a minute later and joined the others around the fire. He talked in a low voice between Tom and Sienna. The fire swelled as it licked at the wood. In the burst of light, Jo could see three pairs of eyes on her.

She couldn't stop shaking, even when she set up her bedroll as far away from the men as she dared. She readied herself for bed and placed her hunting knife right under her pillow for easy access.

"You good?"

Jo jumped, but it was only Nell. She looked curiously at Jo, then back at the fire, like she was checking to see who might be watching. Then, she dropped her pack and unrolled her bed beside Jo's.

Jo tucked her hands under her thighs to still them.

"R-Ruben," she said slowly. "Cornered me."

Nell listened, waiting for more.

"Okay?"

"He didn't really do a-anything," Jo said, rather lamely. Didn't he?

"Just s-said weird stuff. G-got too c-close."

"He *scared* you?" Nell said, not quite unkind. "He's a guy, Jo. I bet he's just messing with you."

Jo's pulse thudded against her ribs. She flexed her fingers until the feeling came back.

Ruben had stepped into her space and her body had answered before her head could catch up. The heat of him. The *smell.* She shifted her bedroll an inch farther away, careful not to touch Nell, and kept her eyes on the ground until the shaking passed.

"Can I give you some advice?" Nell said, easing onto her bedroll and lacing her fingers behind her head. "You gotta stop taking everything so personal."

"P-personal?"

"That's what Sienna keeps saying." Nell shrugged. "It's not about liking everyone. Ruben stinks, but everyone else seems to like him. Example, you could laugh when they say something funny."

"Ruben's n-not funny," Jo scowled.

"It's just how you get through." The fire popped. Nell curled her pale hands around herself. "I really want this. And I know you do, too. Maybe they'll let us both stay."

Jo drew her knees up to her chin. The firelight warmed one side of her face and left the other in shadow.

"You do want this, don't you?" Nell said, pushing herself onto an elbow. "Jo?"

Jo swallowed. Her eyes stayed on the places where the trees pressed in close.

"I…" What *did* she want? Wherever she went, the dark seemed to follow. "I w-want to be left a-alone."

Nell's smile faltered.

"I just think that…" She hesitated, then lowered her voice. "You don't want to be on the wrong side of this."

Jo turned to her.

"W-what does that m-mean?"

Nell pressed her lips together, gaze flicking toward the men laughing by the fire. After a beat, she rolled onto her back.

"Nothing," she said. "Just try to get some sleep."

The camp awoke while it was dark to a thin layer of dew, and there were half-asleep grumblings to get a fire going. They donned all the layers they owned, and Jo stayed wrapped in her bedroll until it was absolutely time to get moving.

"Hope Kettering's still got chickens, I could use some meat," grumbled Sienna, kicking her horse to pick up the pace. She rode up beside Jo and smiled hugely. "Hey, Mute, can you take my horse for the ride back to Burning Well? I'm riding in the truck with the boys."

Jo tensed. Rafael was usually somewhere around to back her up, but he had taken his place at the front of the company.

"C'mon, don't you like horses?" Sienna continued. The way her gums receded always made Jo think she had extra-long teeth. Her voice dropped as she said, "Saw you and Nell cozying up last night."

Nell rode a few horses up, sitting rigid in the saddle. Her braid hung stiff against her back.

Sienna clicked her tongue.

"She's got a future," she said, easy as anything. "Don't get in the way of that."

Jo was glad when Sienna broke off, and instead wondered how they'd have enough to trade Kettering for a truck, as Sienna implied. Fresh gasoline was scarce.

At the start of the apocalypse, Jo and her mother would walk down the old highways, siphoning gas from the vehicles that were abandoned to rot. The lines of buses and cars gave the illusion of a traffic jam without the noise. It was a dangerous job, mostly because there were lots of places for biters to lurk. Despite the danger and low success rate, Jo's mother and father would keep them out there all day only to collect one gallon of gasoline for the generators back at their campsite. It was not worth the trouble.

"If you're itching to jump around so much," called Rafael to Sienna, "you can ride ahead to Kettering and let them know we're nearing. Then you can come back tonight and report."

Sienna rolled her head, her burnt-red curls falling limply from side to side. She barked for Nell to follow and they both broke into a canter, spitting rocks and dirt as they went. As the sun dipped behind the mountain, it cast a final flicker on Ruben's silhouette.

Jo had made sure there were horses between them when the company fell into line but she still anticipated him looking back at her any moment. She braced herself for his black eyes and his wolf's teeth dripping.

Jo hadn't told Rafael about the run-in with Ruben in the woods. Rafael rarely had a moment alone that Jo could take advantage of, but she wasn't even sure that she could explain what had happened. She couldn't come to Rafael with every little thing that made her uncomfortable, but she equally hated that Ruben was more frightening than a biter to her.

12: FRACTURE

The terrain changed with the shift in elevation: the grass was green and thick, and buds poked out of thickets that grew past knee-high. Early spring blossomed as they descended the mountain, but the greenery brought a price.

As they angled toward the valley floor, the smell crept in beneath the green; rot threaded through it, old and patient. Jo saw the first movement near the trees. It could have been a sway of branches, but there was no wind.

She saw shapes half-buried in growth, bodies slowed by cold and vines, a pair of empty sockets.

Jo put her lips together and gave a sharp whistle. Rafael stopped so Ruben nearly ran his horse into him. "Hey–!"

Rafael shushed him, his gaze raking the treeline. "Biters," he warned, quiet and steady. "We keep moving, slowly."

Some of the horses pawed the dirt. A branch cracked somewhere off the path.

Ruben leaned forward in his saddle. "There's only a few," he said, voice too loud. He swung a leg over his mount. "We handle it now, we don't drag them with us."

Rafael grabbed his reins.

"No," he said. "We get to the clearing. We don't stir them up in close quarters."

Ruben wrenched free. His boots hit the mud with a wet sound.

"They're right there," he snapped, fear sharpening his grin as he raised his blade. "You wanna wait till they're on us?"

The horses started to dance, bodies pressing in tight. Jo felt boxed in, one flank breathing hot against her knee, another crowding her from behind. She tightened her grip on the reins and looked to Rafael. He was still mounted, trying to hold the line together with nothing but his voice.

"Stay on your horses," he said. Sharper now. "No one else dismounts."

Ruben had already stepped off the path. He edged toward the brush, machete lifted, peering into the green like he could stare the danger down. Two of the older Wolfskins followed him, muttering under their breaths. The newer recruits stayed put, eyes flicking between Rafael and Ruben, unsure which way to lean.

Rafael wheeled his mount hard.

"I said stay put," he barked, fury breaking through at last. "Get back here, Ruben. Now."

Foliage cracked. One of the biters pushed free of the brush. It dragged one foot, the other bound up in roots that trailed behind it. Its fingers were long, knuckles swollen and split, pale growth curling out of the joints. When it lifted its head, its jaw hung open, packed with vine and dark rot, a wet sound working in the back of its throat as it reached toward the horses.

The line spooked. The horses snorted and sidestepped.

Ruben barked a laugh. "Look at it," he said. "Thing's ancient."

He stepped in before Rafael could stop him. The machete flashed once. The head came free cleanly and dropped into the grass with a dull thud, roots still twitching as the body folded in on itself.

Ruben wiped the blade on his sleeve, grinning. "See?" he said. "Nothing to it."

Rafael swore under his breath. "Move. Now." He dug his heels in and his horse surged forward, forcing the line to follow. One by one the others fell in, hooves finally finding a rhythm as they pushed toward the thinning trees ahead.

Jo exhaled as her horse stepped out from the crush. The path widened and light broke through the canopy. She loosened her grip by a fraction.

Then she glanced back.

Ruben hadn't mounted. He stood just off the trail, blade low, watching her with that grinning look that made her stomach drop.

The brush behind him burst.

A biter lunged from the dark and caught him at the leg. Fingers clamped hard, skin splitting as roots punched through. Ruben shouted and stumbled, his laughter frozen on his face. The machete flashed wildly as he tried to shake it loose. Another shape surged forward, then another, jaws working as they closed the distance.

Ruben went down hard, knee buckling under the weight. He hacked at the thing gripping him, blade biting into shoulder and neck, but it didn't let go. Roots tore wider through its hands as it dragged itself closer, mouth snapping inches from his calf.

"Get back," Rafael shouted. He swung his horse around, gun out. "Everyone back."

Someone fired their weapon too early. The crack echoed off the trees and the sound carried, rolling downhill.

Ruben screamed as the biter's teeth sank in and his leg went rigid beneath it. Rafael dismounted and crossed the distance fast. He grabbed Ruben by the collar and hauled him upright, forcing the biter away with a boot to its chest. Rafael drove his knife down into its skull and leaned his weight into it until the body went slack. He kicked it aside, roots tearing free as it collapsed, then turned back to Ruben without a word.

Ruben shook his head once, breath coming short.

"It's fine," he said, too quick. "Didn't even break the skin—

His hand jerked. The machete slid from his fingers and struck the ground with a dull clang.

Rafael's gaze dropped to Ruben's leg. Jo saw it too, even from where she sat frozen in the saddle. A tight ring of marks bit into the flesh, teeth set neat as a stamp. The skin around it had already gone dark with veins spidering out in black threads. At the center, the flesh bulged and split. Tiny yellow shoots pushed through, tender, like new bud forcing its way up through soil.

Ruben's face folded in on itself.

"Raf," he said, hoarse. Then louder, like volume might fix it. "Raf—don't."

Rafael drew Ruben in close, one hand steady at his shoulder.

"I'm sorry," he said, and looked it.

Ruben spat a curse, cut short by Rafael's knife flashing, quick and practiced. Ruben slacked and collapsed at Rafael's feet.

Jo had watched Rafael put down biters before, but this was a man she'd eaten near. Her stomach lurched. She thought of the way Ruben had loomed over her in the trees, the moment she'd wanted him gone. The thought made her feel worse now, not better. She swallowed and tasted bile.

Around them, a few of the Wolfskins looked away, hands dangling like they'd forgotten what to do with them. Others stayed fixed on Rafael, their eyes burning. Jo saw it then, clear as the bite on Ruben's leg.

This wasn't over.

That night, they made camp along the outskirts of Kettering. The hospital's concrete wings rose above the trees, but no one commented on the vastness of it. The usual noise of chatting and settling wasn't there. Jo watched the shape of the building from the edge of the firelight and felt the earlier certainty drain out of her. Whatever she'd thought this trip would prove no longer seemed clear. After the clearing, after Ruben, it felt like the ground had shifted under all of them, and no one knew yet where to plant their feet.

"How you doing, kiddo?"

Rafael sank onto the log Jo was sitting on. He sat only close enough that his shoulder warmed her sleeve. She breathed easier.

Rafael hadn't touched his dinner: beans and jerky again, and they were almost out of jerky.

"Wish you didn't have to see that," he said, and she could guess what he was referring to.

Jo picked at a splinter in the log.

"I know."

The wind trickled through the trees, and the Wolfskins flinched at any organic sound. Jo watched the fire chew through a knot of pitch until it popped and sent sparks skittering.

"Jo," Rafael said, quieter now. "I want you to do something for me."

He leaned in closer, a miniscule amount, eyes on his men's silhouettes.

"If at any point I tell you to run, you run. No questions."

Her head came up. "Do you think K-Kettering will do something?"

"I'm more worried for Kettering, I think," he murmured.

She frowned.

"Why?"

He rubbed the scar on his knuckle. "Because people don't like to be wrong, and when they've had enough, they'll always make the choices that protect their own."

The Wolfskins had clustered by the fire, talking low, laughing, and cutting it short.

Rafael leaned back, the log creaking.

"You stay near me," he said. "And if I say move, you move."

She nodded, feeling sick.

Hoofbeats cut through the settling quiet, and Sienna rode in hard from the trail with Nell close behind.

Both horses were damp with sweat and breathing hard. Sienna swung down and Nell followed, pulling off her helmet, cheeks flushed from the ride.

"I can't wait for you to see Kettering," Nell whispered, plopping down next to Jo like Sienna hadn't warned her not to. "Their greenhouses are amazing. And they've got real trucks."

Jo didn't answer. She watched Sienna count heads. When Sienna stopped short and asked where the hell Ruben was, Jo felt her stomach tighten, Nell's excitement buzzing distantly beside her.

Rafael stepped forward.

"He was bit," he said.

Sienna stilled. The camp seemed to stop breathing to hear her response, to watch the fight.

"He was bit," She repeated, then pulled her hair off her neck.

"I did what I had to do," said Rafael.

Skepticism flashed across her features.

"You didn't even try to hold him."

Rafael didn't move.

"There wasn't time."

"There's always time," Sienna replied. "You could've tied him up. Bought us a few minutes, at least for me to get back. He was one of my best men."

Rafael's jaw flexed.

"They're all my men," he said. "And my responsibility. One bite risks the whole line. You know that."

Sienna's mouth twitched.

"I know he wasn't done yet."

Someone coughed, loud in the pause.

"I won't gamble lives," Rafael said, hands tight at his sides. "Rules exist so we don't lose more people."

"Funny," she said. "Ruben never had a problem taking risks."

Her gaze slid past Rafael, over the circle of men and lingering on each face before moving on.

"Get some rest," she ordered them. "Big day tomorrow."

She walked off, leaving the fire burning low and the space where Ruben should've been unmistakably empty. Many of the Wolfskins followed her.

Jo lay awake long into the night, watching the sky to see if the stars would move. When the fire burned down to coals and the camp finally stilled, she reached into her boot and slid the thin scrap of paper free. She unfolded it enough to trace the square she knew was Burning Well and the thin line that marked the road they'd taken. Rafael's road. She pressed her thumb there and let herself believe, for a moment, that it was as simple as following it back. Whatever Sienna had meant, whatever Rafael was watching for, would pass them by if they stayed quiet and did things right. She folded the paper again and tucked it away before sleep overtook her.

The next morning dawned under a haze so thick it swallowed the top of Kettering. The night's tension hadn't lifted, only stayed hovering there with the fog. The canopy creaked as the wind moved through it, and the horses shifted, uneasy, leather creaking.

Jo woke with the taste of old fear in her mouth. She pulled on her boots, shrugged into her coat, and made for the stream, watching for crunchy-looking leaves. A bird flapped somewhere above in a snap of wing beats.

As Jo took a drink and wiped her mouth, she realized someone was talking. She combed the surrounding tree trunks with bleary eyes, and through the fog, she could make out three figures in a cluster by the horses.

"C'mon, Sienna. We gotta move before they get up."

"Shut your mouth," Sienna hissed. "They'll hear."

Jo went still. She crouched low with her heart banging, and pressed herself into the brush.

Sienna's voice cut again.

"We do it quick. Rafael's harder to take down without our guns."

"Can't we just pop him once in the head? Make it easier on ourselves?"

"I already told you, no!" Sienna said. "The Kettering soldiers are gone, but there's still a lot of folk in there. If we lose that surprise attack, we can kiss this whole operation goodbye."

"Okay, okay, we go in with the tear gas first. Tom and I will take care of that. And then straight for the armory."

"No, the trucks, idiot. I saw them on the back lot, east side. We roll through Kettering with those, and no one will–"

"Hey," Nell said, after a beat. "Jo's not in her bed."
Jo clapped a hand over her mouth to stop her sharp intake of breath. "Dammit," hissed Tom, his machete gleaming at his side.

Three Wolfskins broke at once, one of them close enough that Jo felt the rush of air as he passed. She had to get to Rafael first.

"Jo!" came Rafael's cry. Jo couldn't pick out where it had come from. There was another cry, and then, "Jo, do what I said. *Now!*"

There was an explosion of activity from the camp, and bodies moved in and out of the mist. There were clanging sounds of a skirmish and shouts of rage. Horses were screaming.

Jo skirted around the clearing, her hunting knife shaking in her fist. Something was burning. She wouldn't run, not yet. She wasn't going anywhere, not without Rafael.

She found him in a heated one-on-one with Sienna, their fists falling and their teeth bared. Rafael swung his rifle around to block the blows from Sienna's machete.

"Traitors!" roared Rafael.

Sienna's eyes glinted with malice as she reached into her belt with an opposite hand, pulled out her gun, and fired.

Rafael stumbled backward, blood pooling from a wound Jo could not pinpoint. There was mild surprise on his face as his brown eyes met Jo's. Then gravity pulled him down hard into the soft grass. He lay still.

Something hot boiled through Jo's insides, and from the deepest caverns of her soul came a scream that ripped her throat in two. She descended on Sienna, her dagger flashing through the air. She felt the jagged blade catch flesh, felt hot blood spatter across her forehead, and she was thrown violently onto her back.

"You little–!"

The sole of her boot fell hard onto her chest, and the air left her lungs as the bite of broken bone cracked in the clearing.

Jo stayed where she was, nose pressed against the dirt, waiting for the sting of Sienna's bullet in her head. It didn't come. The thick ringing in her ears stopped, and the world slowly came back into focus.

Something moved in the fog. That one something became two, then three. In moments, there was a line of figures shambling towards the orange flames.

"Biters!" came the cry.

Jo obeyed the urge to stand, and with Sienna preoccupied with the horde breaking through the trees, she stumbled away, the pain in her side throbbing.

Rafael. She had to get to him and drag him out of there before the horde overtook them. He had just been knocked out, that was all. He was tougher than Sienna, tougher than all of them. He couldn't be…

Nell appeared through the debris and held her gun so Jo was staring down the barrel. "It's…it's not personal," Nell said, her voice quiet.

Rage smoldered in Jo's eyes, and Nell actually flinched. There was a clash of gunshots as the biters arrived amongst Sienna's cries to hold fire. Jo's heart jumped as a rotting face entered her line of vision, yellow fingers outstretched. Nell spun around and unloaded her pistol at the biter.

Jo turned and ran.

She tripped over something fleshy and kept running. Someone was close to her. She could feel the thumps of boots on the broken earth moving fast.

Another gunshot. Another scream. A noise like ripping and an explosion. Had Kettering heard the noise and come to join in the attack?

Nell reached her and growled as she sprang. Her hand brushed Jo's heel, and suddenly vanished into the mist.

Jo ran.

13: ALL GONE

RADIO LOG 37
Location: Ambridge

EZRA: Agh.

Aghh.

Okay, okay. Record, just record.

Ruth's gone. She's just gone. They took her. They just…took her.

It was those cultist freaks from Burning Well, the same ones Roslyn told us about. They came right up to our door in broad daylight like it wasn't…like they weren't…

They offered us some supplies, first. It's always supplies, like we're so poor we should be grateful for it all. They showed us their pretty little weapons and talked about their "amazing" training programs. Which, okay, training programs my ass. No one just "trains" for free. "Oh, such amazing opportunities for young people, the city is so safe, bla bla bla…"

Well, Birdie told them that no one in Ambridge was interested in joining their…their whatever. So they left. It seemed fine, and I thought, great. Good riddance.

They left, but they came back tonight.

[A small crash]

…s-sorry. Dropped the mic. I literally can't stop shaking. But I gotta record this, just so…just so we have a record of these guys and…and what happened. I don't know what I'm doing.

They came in with a truck and cages. Actual cages for animals. They broke the gate clean off its hinges and rushed the place, like they were happy to finally take off the façade…

God. There was so much screaming.

I've never seen Birdie like that. She didn't yell or anything, just…I dunno, she just locked in, was sniping guys with one arm. She was shoving us to safety and told me and Theo to lead the little ones out the back way. I saw her drag someone twice her size out of a cage.

But Ruth…

I didn't see how they got her.

And that's the part that keeps looping over and over in my brain. I was right there. I should've seen it. One second she was behind me, complaining about her boots being too tight. The next—

Judee took some of our guys and went right after them. We have no idea where Burning Well is on the map, so the plan is to follow close behind, and not get caught. I haven't heard from them.

So now I'm here in the shack. Waiting.

I think I've been sitting here for five—no, six?—hours. Hard to tell. The clock stopped ticking at some point. Nothing else to do in here but…keep my hands busy. I've rewired the television a few times already.

Yeah. I gotta keep them busy. If I stop moving, I start thinking. And right now I'm thinking…Burning Well knew exactly where we were and who to take. A lot of younger ones, and women. Ruth…

I feel so bad for Judee. I can't imagine if someone took my sister. I don't have one, but…

Still scares the hell out of me.

If anyone finds this later—if this log survives longer than we do—Burning Well is not safe. I don't care what they promise and I don't care how clean their city looks.

They take people, alive, and they don't bring them back.

Ruth's tough, she always has been.

I have to believe that if Theo and I keep the place running, if we keep the signal up, someone will hear us. Someone can help. Or, I dunno, it'll actually do something.

Okay.

I'm going to keep working. That's all I can do.

[Click]

II: FOOLERY

Foolery, sir, does walk about the orb like the sun, it shines everywhere.

-Shakespeare, *Twelfth Night*

14: AMBRIDGE

Jo had no idea where she was going. Her lungs ached with heavy use, her bones trembled with every press into the earth, and still she ran straight into the white mist. For all she knew, she could have been running in circles, and would arrive back at the wreckage and Nell's gunpoint. In the corner of her vision, Jo thought she saw the flash of Sienna's fiery hair. Jo ran harder until the sharp ends of branches scraped her cheeks raw. A low branch struck her shoulder, and she didn't know she was on the ground until she felt a root poking her back.

She lay there trying to catch her breath, thinking that if Nell was right behind her, she would just have to kill her. Jo didn't have the strength to move. She must have slept because pine needles stuck to her cheek when she raised her head again.

At dawn, Jo walked. She was slow and kept one hand on her ribcage and one on the hilt of her hunting knife. Before night fell, she caught the sounds of dripping and found a small stream winding between the rocks. As she knelt on the bank to drink, she tilted her head and realized she had seen the peculiar path of that stream somewhere before.

She drank until her stomach cramped, then wiped her mouth on her sleeve and stayed there a moment, knees sunk in the mud. When she shifted, her boot pressed wrong against the rock and she remembered the seam she'd sewn into the sole.

Jo pried the leather open and slid the paper free. It uncurled slowly, stiff with damp. Her hands shook as she flattened it against her thigh. The thin line she'd traced so many nights before ran crooked across the page, then dipped. She looked down at the stream. The bend matched, and so did the split where the water narrowed.

Her chest hitched. The markings didn't stop at the wall of Burning Well. The line kept going, deeper into the valley, past places she'd never seen.

Jo folded the map once, tucked it into her coat, and turned to follow the water.

She trudged on for another day and the landscape sloped downward. She walked beside the stream, and according to the rough scribbles, it would soon lead to a sort of archway. From there, a circle. A pond or body of water, Jo figured. Maybe there she could find something to eat, like a rabbit. Just how she was going to trap something with her modest hunting knife still eluded her, but it was a thought that kept her moving.

The mist lifted when she reached the heart of the valley, and the rocks were exchanged for lush greens. Thick grass carpeted the ground, dotted with wildflowers. Jo had never seen the trees so fat with health or foliage dotted with so many varieties of flowering plants. Burning Well kept the plants burned to ash and the trees to blackened stumps. It kept the biters from hanging around.

Immersed in the lushness of greens, Jo felt tight and uneasy.

She kept herself low and as hidden as possible in the underbrush, eyes peeled for berries or wild onions. While she combed the dirt with her fingers, a thick breeze blew in from the trees, and the sound of rustling along with it. Things were moving, but not a herd of wild deer or a flock of birds. It looked like the trees themselves were shifting.

Jo froze with her hand outstretched, and squinted to peer into the darkness.

There were shapes of human outlines, but nothing about them moved the way biters did. The bodies had softened with rot and time, then been overtaken by growth. Leaves poured from shoulders and hips. Moss quilted their chests and backs, and vines threaded through their ribs and coiled along their arms, blooming there.

They stood together and swayed with the breeze, faces angled toward the thin light filtering through the canopy. Jo felt the old fear tighten her chest all the same. It sat beside something else she didn't trust, a pull she couldn't name, brought on by the way death here refused to be simple.

She moved on from that place quickly.

As she stole around clearings and avoided the soft chorus of the biters, Jo tripped over one of them. She scrambled away, blade raised, and she saw that the biter did not move. The shape of it was there—four limbs and a head connected to a torso shape—but it had the appearance of something growing out of the ground. It lay flat, fingers stretching root-like into the dirt, eyes just two open pits, gaping mouth sprouting with green bulbs. It lay at the base of a budding tree with baby branches. It was still.

Jo had never seen a biter reach the stage of death, if that was the word for it. She didn't know if the parasite died along with it—it needed a living host. Burning Well had its wandering biters, but they usually reached their end with a quick shot of a pistol. She'd never heard of a biter lying down to let the earth claim it.

The canopy-dimmed sunlight faded, and Jo knew she'd have to find a safe place to rest before a biter caught sight of her. She didn't think she would have the strength to fight one off.

Then, peeking between the trees, a shape made of white-washed stone entered her line of vision. It was an archway standing barren, its walls long since crumbled away.

Jo heard a sound like fabric tearing underwater. It stopped her mid-step, the noise spreading through the trees and flattening against the trunks. For a moment she swayed, disoriented. The woods looked the same in every direction. Damp air pressed close. The sound wavered again, low and insistent, buzzing in a way that set her teeth on edge.

Then the smell hit.

A biter stood inches from her, its jaw rotted down to a hinge, the rest gone. The noise in its throat rasped and scraped, close enough that she felt it in her chest. One hand reached for her, fingers mostly eaten away, the grip weak but certain.

Her body locked. She couldn't move.
The creature drew its head back to bite when the butt of a hammer crashed through its head. Something black and sticky rained out, and the biter slumped forward, dead-standing.

Jo was aware of falling, of hitting the ground. She heard the ripping sound again, knowing she had heard it once before.

Jo's eyes fell out of focus, and the sight of a person was exchanged for darkness.

Jo opened her eyes to a square window looking out onto a black night. She realized that she was lying on a mat against a wall, and could still feel the cold floor through its padding. It took her a moment to see that someone was in the dark with her.

"So you're awake," they said.

A woman was sitting by the fireplace. Her long, tattooed limbs poked out of the dark. As she struck a match, Jo could make out tanned, sun-speckled skin and a shaved head pricked with ink writing. The taught grooves in her skin betrayed some age, perhaps forties, but everyone looked older than they were these days.

Though her limbs were thin, she looked strong in the way she picked up a log and thrust it into the stove grate. Light filled the damp space.

"Y'know, you could've said you were thirsty. Woulda saved Ezra the trouble of carrying you back here, anyway," she said.

She stuck out her foot and prodded something towards Jo's bedside. It scraped along the stone, and Jo could see that it was a cup of water and a bowl.

Jo drank the water in two gulps and slurped the weak stew. She could feel it pass through her chest and into the empty cavern of her stomach. The woman watched her, but Jo didn't have the strength to be self-conscious.

"You're not infected," the woman said. "That's good. I'm surprised the biters didn't get you sooner, you being in your shape."

She leaned forward so light danced over the bump of her brow.

"I'm Judee. What should I call you?"

When Jo didn't answer, the woman continued.

"We don't see a lot of people come near Ambridge. Why were you wandering around the arch?"

Jo bit her lip.

"You a scout or something? You lose your group? Where're your people? Why don't you talk?"

Jo heaved a breath, which hurt, and coughed out a sob. She couldn't help it. The memory of Rafael lying in the grass, blood pooling from his gut…

"Stop. Geez. Don't cry."

Jo swiped the wetness from her eyes with the back of her hand, but her breath pulled harshly at her throat. She had to think.

"Where a-a-am I?" Jo asked. The sound of her own voice startled her. It was hoarse from disuse.

"So you *can* talk," Judee replied. "I was starting to worry I was yacking while you were hard of hearing or something."

Jo searched the woman's face for a trace of deception, but the woman merely looked curious.

"Ezra found you and a biter going head-to-head," continued Judee, reaching a long arm over to refill Jo's water cup. "You seemed like you'd been through it, so he had me take a look at you."

While Judee talked, Jo took in her surroundings more closely, searching for bars on the windows, perhaps someone hiding in the shadows. But the cabin was quiet save for Judee's voice and the snapping of the fire.

"You d-didn't t-tie me up," Jo said, surprised.

"I did."

It was then that Jo heard a soft clinking noise, and finally noticed the chain enclosed on her left ankle.

"Even if I didn't, it doesn't look like you're going anywhere," Judee said. "You've got three fractured ribs.

Jo planted her palms on the mat and pushed, but her lungs ached with the pressure. She slumped back.

"I'm a doctor," said Judee, which Jo guessed was supposed to be comforting. "Well, close enough to."

As Judee wiped her hands on her apron, Jo's eye caught on a small gray box clipped to her belt. It was scuffed and familiar, the same size and shape as the one she'd found at the campground. The one that had hissed in the woods. The one with the paper hidden inside.

Judee stood up and waved a ring of keys in the air.

"Time to go," she said. "Some folks wanna talk to you."

The path underfoot was packed and familiar, worn smooth by traffic. Judee's lantern glowed orange against the backdrop of stars, and shapes of buildings rose up on both sides like two clefts closing in.

Jo kept her eyes darting. She'd heard stories about towns like this, about who survived behind walls and what they took to keep them fed. She gauged distances, exits, the weight of the chain. She could run…and then what? She wasn't going back to Burning Well if she could help it.

And Rafael…

If he was dead—which she had to consider, there was no point denying it—what would she do? Where was home?

The path bent and a wall rose ahead, timber and scrap stacked high. Gates stood open long enough to let them through, then shut again behind them with a solid thud.

Judee stopped at a large log cabin and rapped once, hard.

"It's me," she called. "I've got the stray."

The door opened, and Judee tugged her inside.

There was a fire roaring in the room's main grate and tables set on sun-faded carpets, wooden shelves along the walls piled with stacks of folders and crates labeled with things like "Tools" and "Craft" and "R&R." Couches sagged in a loose semi-circle.

Judee knocked on a second door and went in without waiting. The room beyond was a makeshift office, lit by an electrical desk lamp that actually worked. The woman behind the desk was built like a bull, hair braided in black and silver down her shoulders.

"We've got enough HQ workers," she said.

"This is the one Ezra found in the woods, Birdie," Judee said. "Looked rough when he picked her up."

She dropped her voice.

"She was alone. Hasn't said much. I don't know."

Birdie looked Jo up and down, and there was something behind her hard eyes that flickered briefly.

She adjusted her sleeve so Jo could plainly see the diagonal cut just above the place where Birdie's elbow used to hang. The skin was lumpy there, but whole.

"I got bit," Birdie said, in answer to Jo's staring. "Had to chop it off before the infection set in. Sometimes you gotta get rid of the things that ain't serving you."

It was a last-ditch action people talked about, but Jo had never seen it work. There were stories about someone chopping off a limb in hopes of stopping the parasite from taking root. Either the parasite won anyway, or the person bled out before they had a chance.

"She's from Burning Well," Judee said.

"How do you know that?" said Birdie sharply.

Judee lifted the map into the lamplight. Of course she'd taken it.

"Judee," Birdie said slowly, squinting. "That's... that's yours, ain't it?"

Judee nodded.

"Made it when we went after Ruth. Lost it when the biters jumped us." Her eyes slid back to Jo. "Where's the radio, kid?"

Ruth?

"You found this inside the casing," Judee went on. "I know you did. That's where I kept it."

She stepped closer.

"So where's the radio? Did you hand it to your general? Did he send you in here first to look us over?"

Her hand fisted in Jo's shirt, yanking her forward.

"Does he want more brides? Was Ruth not enough?"

The name hit like a blow.

"I—" Jo winced as pain flared through her ribs. "I kn-knew h-her."

Judee froze. Then she shook Jo hard, like she was trying to wake her.

"What do you mean?"

Jo swallowed hard, the memory of Ruth's soft, determined face returning to the front of her mind.

"B-brides," Jo managed, and Judee audibly gasped at the word.

"We w-were in the t-tower together."

"Where is she now?" Judee demanded. "You got out, didn't you? Did she?"

Jo's head swam. Judee's hands clamped down on her shoulders and she stared, searching Jo's face for something she wouldn't give. Saying Ruth had turned wouldn't change anything, and wouldn't bring her back.

"Judee," Birdie said quietly. "Ruth's gone. Ain't she?"

Jo nodded until Judee let her go to throw the desk chair against the wall hard enough to splinter the paneling. Judee pressed her forehead into the crook of her arm, her shoulders hitching as she sobbed. Jo stood there and said nothing, holding the rest of it inside where it couldn't hurt anyone else.

"I'm sure you know this, Burning Well girl," Birdie said after a minute. "But years back, your people came in and took ours. Took Ruth. Put her in a truck and hauled her straight to your General."

Jo swallowed hard, but the lump in her throat had closed the dam on her voice. She knew that there were cases of the Wolfskins bringing people back to Burning Well. Ruth was one of them, and Billie and Washington. But everyone else had been invited or coerced. The people-snatching had stopped when Rafael became Captain. Things were different now, he always said.

Except things weren't different. The very taste of Burning Well was sour in Jo's mouth.

"People don't usually run from that place," Birdie went on.

"Especially not brides."

The memory of the fight burned in Jo's memory, and Jo found her throat tighten as images of Rafael, blood, and horses screaming and smoke.

Jo's throat closed. She fixed her eyes on the floorboards, willing the room to narrow until there was nothing left to see.

"Talk!" Judee demanded, tears brimming in her eyes. "What's wrong with you?" Jo didn't answer. She couldn't.

Birdie nudged the splintered chair pieces out of the way with her boot and leaned toward Judee, her voice low. Whatever she said didn't carry.

"Yeah, I know," Judee snapped back. "So what? We're all wrecked. I don't want her here."

Birdie turned back to Jo. Studying her for a moment.

"One more time," she said. "Did they hurt you in Burning Well? You don't gotta say it, a nod or a shake is fine."

Jo nodded.

"You were," Judee glanced at Birdie, "a bride, too?"

Jo swallowed and nodded once.

"Did you run?" Another nod.

"Were you followed?" Jo shook her head.

It wasn't true, but it was safer than the truth, and right now, safety mattered more than honesty.

Jo stayed at Judee's cottage and slept another day. Judee interacted to help change bandages and feed, but otherwise, she was gone.

Jo was left untied, but it wasn't like she had anywhere else to go. And they were feeding her. That was something. As Jo fell in and out of consciousness, she listened to the bustle outside the door: voices, some hammering, and once she thought, music.

Late one evening, Judee came back to the cabin. She kicked off her mud-caked boots and draped her arm over her eyes.

"Cooooome in, Saint Jude. This is HQ. Please be so kind as to give us your status. Over."

Jo jumped at the harsh ripping sound coming from the radio on Judee's hip. Without uncovering her eyes, Judee pressed the button on her walkie so it clicked.

"This is Judee," she said. "Home safe and sound. Wasn't followed. No bites and no biters in sight. Over."

"Aaall righty, Saint Jude, get some sleep. Sandlot is taking over the rest of the night watch, and you're due to report first thing in the morning, bright and early. Over."

"We need to train more people for this stuff, Ezra," Judee groaned and flopped back on the bed. "My shot sucks in the dark, and I've got enough on my plate. Trying to cobble together medicines with sticks and leaves, but we're gonna need the real stuff in case someone gets a real injury. Plus I've gotta watch the invalid. Over."

"Don't use my name. It's 'Prophet'. Over."

"No one is listening in, kid," Judee grunted. "Unless they're crouching outside my window. Over."

"Owl told me to ask how the stray is doing. Over."

Judee popped off her mattress and dipped back outside to get some privacy. Only when she strained, Jo was just able to hear Judee utter,

"I've been watching her like a hawk, but she's quiet. Just stopped talking out of nowhere. Hasn't snooped, hasn't tried to leave. She doesn't talk much to me, but Birdie—sorry, *Owl*—said that's to be expected coming from Burning Well." She sighed, lowering her voice. "What was she...did she say anything when you first found her? Over."

"No. She was in bad shape and could barely keep her eyes open. At one point I thought I was carrying a dead body. She looked...bad. Someone didn't like her, that's for sure. Over."

"Kind of like when we picked you and your brother up, huh? Y'all were so caked in mud we thought you were swamp things. Over."

"Oh, hey, I'm sorry about your sister. We were all hoping that Ruth...well, it just sucks. It sucks every time. Over."

"Yeah," Judee said at length. "Part of me hoped...I dunno. I left my radio outside the wall, hoping that she would find the map inside and come home. Over."

"Hey, you did what any of us would have done. I'm just sorry. Seriously."

A pause.

"People are getting curious, asking who I found in the woods. Will the Burning Well girl be off soon, d'you think? Over."

"If she was a threat, we'd know by now," said Judee. "But I dunno. She can leave once she's feeling better, if she wants. I don't care. Over."

"Yup, just release her into the wild, where it's safe and sound. That's humane to me. Over."

"Oh, and come find me tomorrow. Owl and I got some books for you to take to the library since you're already heading that way."

There was a yawn, Jo could hear from inside.

"Listen, I gotta turn in, kid," Judee said. "Early day tomorrow. Over and out."

"Aw, c'mooon. I gotta sit here all night and man the radio, I'm gonna go crazy all by myself. It gets creepy here at night. Over."

"Just bother someone else's radio. You love doing that. Over and out."

"Aaaall righty, friends, that's gonna do it for us. You're listening to Ambridge 103.7, and be sure to tune in next time to find out why our beloved grandma Jude has such a massive stick up her butt."

"Over and *out*, Ezra."

When Judee came back inside she tossed the radio onto the table.

"Pain in my ass," she grumbled. "Thinks he's a damn radio host."

It was the image of the radio that kept Jo awake that night. She thought about squashing the hope that Rafael was alive. It was too risky to hope for that. Hope was such a fluffy, poorly defined thing, a vague wish for a miracle. But at that moment, there was nothing vague about it.

There was real, tangible, solid hope that Rafael had his radio when she'd lost him in the glen.

Judee's snores permeated the room, and Jo stared at the ceiling in the dark, the corners of her eyes burning.

Jo suspected that Judee was tired of babysitting because she dropped Jo off at HQ before the sun was up. Just as well. Jo hadn't slept anyway, and she thought headquarters would have answers.

Birdie met her in the hall. Judee must've called ahead on one of those radios. Birdie yawned wide, her jaw stretching like a bear's, and motioned Jo toward the fire grate. She sat heavily and rubbed at her face.

"Afraid we can't do better than dandelion tea," she said, handing Jo a tin mug.

The liquid was bitter and hot. Jo wrapped both hands around it.

"I've been wanting to ask you something, Burning Well girl," Birdie said after a moment.

She leaned forward, one elbow on her knee, her severed forearm hanging above the other.

"We've given you time. How'd you get out?"

Jo cradled her cup, her fingernails scraping against the metal.

"I know your General doesn't let people walk away," Birdie went on. "So I'm guessing it wasn't smooth."

Birdie then reached down and slid something across her knee. A water-stained pad of paper and a charcoal pencil.

"Might be easier than talking," she said. "Sometimes things happen and take something with them."

Jo's eyes flicked, despite herself, to Birdie's arm.

"Doesn't mean you can't still work," Birdie added, with a small smirk.

Jo ran her palm over the paper. When she wrote, she kept it simple. She drew in the margins where words failed her. When she finished, she handed the pad back and wiped her blackened fingers on her pants.

Birdie read without comment. When she was done, she leaned back with a grunt and tapped the paper once.

"Haven't heard this one before," she said. "You heading out soon? To look for your pop?"

Jo shrugged.

"Hope's a stubborn thing," she said. "But I wouldn't advise going alone. Especially with the rains coming. You've seen what grows in the valley."

Jo took a sip and burned her tongue.

"If I were you," Birdie continued, "I'd ask around first. Suncrest or Roslyn. Someone might've seen something."

Jo picked up the pencil again and wrote: *You think they would have seen him?*

Birdie snorted softly.

"We saw you, didn't we?"

Birdie drained the last of her tea, slapped her knee, and stood.

"This actually solves a problem for me," Birdie went on.

"Ezra's been pestering for an assignment partner. No one goes out alone here. That's a rule. But no one's volunteered."

Her eyes glinted down at Jo.

"You interested?"

Jo nodded, slow.

"You can shoot?" Jo nodded again.

"Good," Birdie said. "Burning Well trains their people mean. Kid'll need someone watching his back."

She stepped closer and took Jo's empty mug.

Jo tapped the pad once more and wrote, smaller this time: Why'd you let me stay?

"You told us about Ruth," Birdie replied. "You didn't have to."

Birdie snatched Jo's mug and finished the cold dregs of tea.

"Judee's mad, but not at you. Wouldn't take that personal."

Jo scribbled another line: *How do you know I'm not a spy?*

Birdie handed the cup back.

"Because," she said, "you don't get three broken ribs unless you pissed somebody off real bad.

15: MEND

Jo went to find Ezra that afternoon, following Birdie's instructions through Ambridge, the notepad pressed against her chest. She walked behind houses and shanties. The brick foundations had withstood the weather, and Jo could pinpoint spots where the residents had connected houses with wooden paths above the street. The slanted roofs looked scrappy, and Jo could see the panels were interwoven with patches of dirt and tiny sprouts.

Gardens on the roof?

Ambridge lacked the secure concrete walls of Burning Well, and Jo felt exposed as she hunched along.

She came to the outskirts of the main village and followed the path around a bend. Jo squinted up the hill and at first thought she was looking at a strange tangle of trees. As she got closer, she could see that it was a steel skeleton sticking up through the clearing.

Jo had seen radio towers in passing. They looked like scaffolding—useless criss-crossed steel beams that didn't do anything other than offer something to climb if biters got too close.

This one had a tiny wood house sitting at its base, about the size of a garden shed, red paint faded and peeling. There was a whole manner of things sticking out from the slanted roof: antennae and pokey-spikes, and a tiny torn flag that read *Comms Center* in yellow paint. It flapped gently in the breeze.

As Jo approached, she saw that someone was sitting outside at the picnic table, hands tangled in black cords and a look of determination set behind a pair of glasses.

Jo stood at the table for almost a full minute before he seemed to notice she was there.

"Ah!" He jumped up, and Jo was met with wild green eyes and a head of curly hair.

He had a young face, and couldn't have been much older than she, though he stood at least a head taller.

"Geez, make a noise or something!"

He was squinting at her as if she was a species of bug he'd never seen before.

"Oh. It's you," he said. "You look way different than when I picked you up. Much less, uh, covered in dirt and blood. But, hey, glad to see you in one piece. And you're from Burning Well, huh?" He didn't wait for an answer. "Not to perpetuate gossip or anything, but it's all we've been talking about on the walkies. Word travels fast and all that."

He whistled.

"You must be well-trained then, huh? That's what they say BW is known for. Can you kill a person with your bare hands? Just a joke."

Listening to him talk made something click in Jo's brain. She realized his was the voice she'd heard on Judee's radio the other night. He'd called himself "Prophet," though the title seemed a little esteemed for the gangly boy standing before her.

"I'm Ezra! Comms Operator," he said, as if reading her mind. "Nice to meet you while you're not completely out of it, Burning Well Girl."

He stuck out his hand under Jo's nose and she took it uncertainly. His handshake was firm, and when she pulled back her palm was smudged with grease.

"You got a name?" He went on as she wiped her hand on her jeans. "No one's told me what it is yet."

He gazed at her behind his glasses and, unwilling to reveal her stammer, Jo scribbled her name on the notepad and thrust it at him.

"Jo," he read, looking from the paper to her face as if expecting her to explain. She didn't. "Jo. Hm. Is that short for something?"

She wasn't sure if he'd meant to be rude, but it sure sounded like it.

"It's nice though," he said. "Just the one syllable."

Ezra handed back the notepad and settled back down at his table.

"She may not have told me your name, but Birdie mentioned that you wanted to join the trip to Roslyn. You're gonna have to help me carry some stuff, just so you know."

She sat on the opposite end of the picnic table and watched him work. He was butchering a wide, metal box. His skinny arms quivered with the effort of loosening one of the rusted screws.

He stopped mid-detangle and furrowed his brow.

"Can I ask why you're so interested in coming along? Just wanna see the sights, or…?"

Lost someone, Jo wrote. *Looking for him.*

Ezra glanced at her scribble.

"I, uh, don't want to get your hopes too high," he said, frowning. "Can you hand me the pliers?"

Jo handed him the pliers. Then she wrote again. *He had one of your radios.*

"Heard about that, yeah."

Can I contact him?

"Our signal stays strictly in Ambridge," said Ezra. After a moment he continued more gently, "Sorry. That's just as far as it goes. We've only got the one tower."

That figured.

"But, I mean, with more towers up and running in Roslyn and Suncrest, that could help your predicament," he said. "It's my theory, anyway."

Ezra pushed his glasses up his nose and tugged at a wire.

"Our three towns make a triangle. Once those towers are up, it should—"

The box sparked, bright and white. Ezra yipped.

"Shit–" Ezra lurched forward, hands flying as he slapped the side of the casing and yanked the wire free. "Okay. Okay. That's on me. That one's on me."

He crouched over it, muttering, curls falling into his face.

"It's fine, mostly. Old wiring. Temperamental." He wiped his hands on his pants and took a breath. "Point is, more towers means more reach."

So, once he built more of those radio towers, there was a chance she could try Raf's radio. When he finished tightening the last screw, she wrote one final line and slid it across the table.

When do we leave?

Ezra read it.

"Soon as I can make this thing stop trying to kill us," he said.

Jo nodded her understanding, tucked the notepad under her arm, and stood carefully, one hand on her ribs.

Ezra made a flinching movement, like he meant to help her, but didn't.

"Uh—yeah. I'll come find you." She left him there with the box, the tower humming faintly overhead.

Jo was tempted to eat dinner alone in Judee's cabin again, but Ezra insisted on her joining him in the mess hall. So, she followed him to the pavilion and tried to ignore the stares.

Ezra talked to everyone they crossed, which didn't help Jo's attempts to stay under the radar. There was laughter in the soup line while Jo tried to make herself small. It got much worse when Ezra started introducing her around: another curly-haired boy named Theo, someone named Stewart or something, and someone who either played the violin or the banjo. Ezra finally gave up when Jo inhaled her food in two monstrous bites and excused herself back to the cabin.

There just wasn't time to get friendly.

Jo didn't sleep that night before the journey. As the moon blazed bright through the square window and Judee's snores filled the house, Jo went over the tattered land map she'd borrowed from the town hall. With the pencil and notepad Birdie had given her, she copied a rough scribble of the land and everything she knew from the Wolfskins' journey to Kettering. She marked known civilizations with X's and then everything else she remembered from the path taken. She marked the possible spot where the mutiny had taken place, and tried to map Rafael's possible journey to Roslyn, had he made it that far.

She shoved aside the image of his glassy eyes. Instead, she clung harder to the path marked out with a defiant line.

Jo stepped into the dewy morning and walked to HQ. Ezra was yawning on the steps and nodded wordlessly when he saw her. Quiet for the first time since she met him, they worked in sleepy silence to pack up his supplies and shoulder their packs. Most of his belongings consisted of coils of copper wire, various tools, a small firearm, a first aid kit, some camping gear, and a bow which he slung over one shoulder. He handed her a backpack that cut into her shoulders and she steadied herself upright, testing the pain in her side. Her injury had healed considerably, and she would be fine as long as she was careful.

Judee was there to see them off and distribute rations. As she dropped the sealed packs into Jo's arms, she set a small, plastic jar on the top.

"It's a salve I made," Judee said. "To help with any discomfort in the ribs."

Jo felt caught off-guard by the gesture.

"I was a dick," Judee said, shifting her weight. "I just…"
Jo licked her lips.

"I-I'm s-s-sorry ab-bout R-R-R…"

She knew her unused voice sounded awful, but Judee watched her with patience. Her razor-hard features softened.

"I'm sorry about Ruth, too," Judee mumbled. "You better get going, or Ezra will leave without you."

The dull orange sun crept into existence, and Jo and Ezra set off on foot. Soon the familiar tips of the Ambridge fence disappeared into the trees.

Spring was in full bloom and it spilled all over the pathway. Jo was prepared to take the journey in silence, content to focus on the road and keep an eye out for biters. She should have counted on Ezra's chatter.

"It'll be cool to see what Suncrest has been up to. You ever seen a play before?" Ezra asked her, and without waiting for her to nod or shake her head—he seemed to assume she was listening—he went on, "Suncrest has this troupe, y'know, a group of actors, and every year they put on a play. I'm a Shakespeare man, myself, which is perfect because they do a totally botched job of all his stuff. It's entertaining, for sure. They once did a version of *The Tempest* with aliens. Wacky. I helped do the rigging on that one."

"You'll really like the library, I think," he continued when they stopped to refill their water canteens in the river. "I saw you looking through some of the stuff at HQ. You must have read everything in there a hundred times already, but just wait till you see what the library's got—"

When they camped for the night, Jo relished in the silence, and dreamed fretfully of Nell poking her shotgun through the trees.

Roslyn was a two-day walk downhill, so Ezra led the way along the curve of the riverbed, prattling lightly. They walked along the river's path and rain plunked gently on the water's surface. Then it came down in sheets. Their shoes squelched as the mud sucked them into the earth with every step.

"Great," Ezra said, head tilted back so water pelted his glasses. "Just peachy."

Sometimes Jo could smell biters before she saw them. The stench of rot and dirt irritated her nose. It took Ezra a few long seconds to realize that she'd halted in the middle of the path.

"What's up?" he asked, pivoting.

Jo strained her ears to listen. A minute went by in rare silence, then Ezra shifted his weight anxiously from foot to foot.

"We should get out of the rain, don't you think?" he asked.

Jo shushed him sharply and it was not a moment too soon, because a chorus of rustling reached her ears, and Jo could feel the hair on her arms stand on end.

Biters, and they were close.

Jo unsheathed her hunting knife and scanned the surrounding trees for movement. Ezra had his gun in both hands, his eyes bugging behind his glasses.

"Ooh-kay, how d'you wanna do this? We could pop them off quickly, but the gun's loud, so I dunno how great it'll be to make a noise in the middle of—"

Jo bit the inside of her cheek and edged down the path, keeping to the center where the ground was clear. The rain masked her steps. Ezra's voice didn't.

"Yup, uh-huh, I like where your head's at! Running away is always an option," Ezra was saying.

He was still talking, still loud.

Jo looked once at the trees, then back at him. She couldn't pull him with her without drawing them all, and she couldn't stop him from talking.

Ezra was already doing it.

She slipped into the brush while he continued to make noise.

It wasn't long before the biters grew more curious as they became fueled and fat with rain. They were sloshing thickly in the surrounding trees, and before long, the shadows took shape and emerged, mouths slack, eye sockets empty, mud-dripping hands outstretched.

"Aaaand there you are!" Ezra yelped.

Ezra's voice held them. The biters leaned toward the sound, shoulders rolling, feet dragging. Jo moved wide, circling through wet brush until the backs of the creatures filled her vision.

"Oooh kay, meatbags," he taunted, his voice steady despite his shaking hand. "There's three of you, huh? Not a problem, not a problem. You guys are slow, anyway. Look at you, shambling along—is that an arm missing, my friend? Yeah, that's what I thought. Uhhh, hey? Jo?"

His head whipped around, his voice rising in pitch.

"Where did you go?!"

The biters followed Ezra as he stumbled back, drawn to the sound and the movement. Ezra shouted and his foot slid in the mud.

He fired his weapon.

Rafael had always taught her that shooting a weapon was a last resort, or making any kind of sudden, loud noise. There were more things to worry about than biters.

One of the biter's heads exploded. Foul blood rained over her face and head. She launched herself back, sputtering, heart hammering and ears ringing from the shot.

When she'd regained her senses, Jo brought her foot down hard on the backs of one of the biters' knees, and the brittle bones shattered. She narrowly dodged its deadly breath, so close she could see yellow curls clawing up from the chasm of its throat. Jo yanked her blade back and sunk it into the biter's skull with finality. She could hear the rain pittering softly again.

Ezra was panting, still gripping his smoking pistol.

"We... I..." he stammered. Rain glistened on his forehead so curls of dark hair stuck there.

Jo wiped her blade hard against the grass and turned away, already moving back down the path. They'd have to move quickly in case other biters grew curious about the sudden pop of Ezra's gun.

"I swear, I didn't see you back there," Ezra explained, falling into step beside her. "What was I supposed to do? I panicked."

Jo looked past Ezra's sweaty face. The rain was making it hard to see. Ezra stepped into her path and spread his arms indignantly.

"You used me," he said.

Jo finally looked at him, unable to hide her own outrage in the grit of her teeth. Stupid of him to fire a weapon when she had been handling it. People five miles away would have heard that shot. And stupid of him to shoot at all. He'd almost killed her.

Ezra blinked down at his pistol, shakily flipped the safety back on.

"You could have said something," he went on. "You could have, I dunno, *communicated* that you were sneaking up behind it, or that you *weren't* just abandoning me to die. Of *course* I fired. I'm not some super soldier like you."

He wiped his glasses, eyes big and hurt.

"I thought you'd left me."

Jo had learned to avoid conflict where she could. It was how she'd survived as long as she did. Her sense of logic kept her alive in situations that would have killed a less practical person. Her mind was one of clear definitions and little overlap.

Ezra would not let her look away, and she didn't completely trust herself to open her mouth and talk.

They camped again only when it was too dark to see. Jo found an overhanging cliff, and they curled up there without a fire to keep them warm.

16: ROSLYN

Roslyn sat lower than Ambridge, framed by pale trees that hadn't yet pushed out their spring leaves. Its outer wall was red brick, cracked in places but solid. When the sun finally broke through the cloud cover, it caught on the stone as Jo and Ezra knocked at the gate.

There was a heavy clunk, and the doors rolled open. Jo clocked the thickness of them as they stepped through and thought of Burning Well's steel walls. She remembered Rafael talking about how much General Hayes wanted a gate like this one. Now she understood why.

The gatekeeper waved them inside and shut the doors at once. He kept his rifle tucked close as he checked them for bites.

"Didn't meet any strange folk on the road, did you?"

"No," Ezra said. "Just the usual undead riffraff. Why?"

"We saw some of Burning Well's wolves slinking around our perimeter the other night," the man replied. "Then movement in the woods after. Didn't have a way to warn you off."

The word made Jo's throat tighten. *Wolfskins.* She pictured Sienna's grin, Nell's stiff posture in the saddle, the group splitting apart before they'd reached their destination. If they'd come this way, there was a chance Rafael had too.

Once they were cleared, they headed toward the library. Roslyn felt old in a way Burning Well never had. The buildings were made with stone and fixed up with wood, giving an overall appearance of old and new colliding.

Ezra walked a step ahead of her. He hadn't said much since the road, and the silence sat wrong on him.

Jo felt it anyway, a thin, persistent discomfort she couldn't shake.

The library sat directly in the center of Roslyn; its circular steeple above all the other rooftops in town. The roof was brown and the outside white, save for one wall that exploded with color: paint in hues of red and gold and blue and green. The image of an ocean wave stretched along the wall and followed the entire length of the concrete. Jo couldn't remember seeing such vivid colors anywhere in Burning Well. The heavy doors were scarred, and Jo tried not to imagine people clawing for sanctuary in the early days of the apocalypse.

Ezra dropped his pack on the ground as soon as they entered through the front doors, and Jo looked around with wide, drinking eyes.

The shelves were sparse but neatly kept. The bookshelves stood tall like guardians and the air carried a scent of aged paper and polished wood. Gold beams of light slanted through the high circular windows. A hushed stillness wrapped around the place, broken only by the faint rustling of pages and the whisper of footsteps treading on carpeted floors.

They passed a heavily locked room with a scratched plaque that read, "Chief Librarian." Through the bars, Jo could see boxes stacked high with paper, drawing materials, snacks and canned goods, hygiene supplies, water bottles, and camp gear. Jo later found out that most supplies were donated, and she had a hard time believing that a place so well-stocked had not been raided. It was just the sort of place Hayes would have loved to get his hands on.

The front of the desk looked wall-papered with loud fliers, round stickers, and yellowing notebook paper. Upon closer inspection, Jo could read the graffitied notes scribbled with things like, "This is a Safe Place" and "No One Messes with the Library," plus a handful of drawings featuring games of hangman and crude pictures of wolves with X'd out eyes.

There was a scroll tacked up on the wall with words written in smudged ink of varying colors, as though it was a list that updated regularly. It read:

WELCOME
-Be respectful of others at all times.
-All visitors must sign in.
-Please check-in all donations to the Chief Librarian.
-There is no fighting in the library.
-Books may not be removed from the premises.
**However, copies may be taken off the premises and distributed beyond the library.*
***Making copies is encouraged.*

Ezra pushed past Jo to help an elderly man lift a box onto the top of the desk.

"Geez, what's in there, Norm?" grunted Ezra. "Bricks?"

"Paper," the librarian replied. He had a proud face and a hooked nose that looked primed for poking into other people's business. He grunted and straightened his back. "You're back to get the radio tower running, are you?"

"That's the plan," Ezra said.

"Good. I'm getting tired of projecting across the square," said the librarian.

Ezra adjusted his pack and without looking at Jo, said, "I'm gonna get started on the tower. It's easier to do by myself, honestly. Maybe you could give Norman a hand here in the meantime."

As he turned on his heel and marched back out the library doors, for once, Jo felt moved to say something. She'd done what she had to do to save them both. He should have seen that.

But the truth was, she was bewildered at how much it seemed to bother him. And more bewildering, that it bothered her, too.

"Keep up, then," said the librarian briskly. "You look like you could lift a box of paper."

Jo stayed in the library that first night. Norman put her to work restocking shelves, and she didn't argue. He and the other librarians didn't ask much, which suited her fine.

Norman talked while they worked. He sorted papers into neat stacks and told stories as if they were part of the catalog. He mentioned a woman who'd wandered in once, shaking and a little out of her right mind. He'd handed her a pile of picture books and let her sit on the floor turning pages until her caretaker found her. Later, he said, they'd discovered a scrap of paper in her pocket with six words written on it: *the library is a safe place.*

Jo slid a row of notebooks into place and thought of Burning Well, where nothing waited for you unless it was meant to be taken.

Norman left her at the shelves to help a visitor. Jo heard the man before she saw him: heavy boots and the scrape of armor. He crossed the room and dropped something onto the front desk hard enough to make the lamps rattle.

Jo paused, one book still in her hand, and looked up.

"Our library had two copies of this," the man said. He set the book on the desk with a dull thud. "Figured you could use one."

Norman peered at the cover over his readers.

"The Souderton branch? You came fifty miles to return a book?"

"Yeah. And, uh—" The man shifted, leather creaking.

"You got the Robot Detective series? Book two? We've only got one and three. I was hopin' to grab it for my—" He cleared his throat, "for my kid."

Norman smiled and reached for the catalog.

By the end of the day, Jo knew Rafael hadn't passed through Roslyn.

She asked the librarians and showed her notepad at the front desk. She walked to the gate and waited until the guards noticed her hovering. On her last scrap of paper, she wrote his name and slid it across the counter. She even drew his beard.

No one had seen him.

The sun set, and one of the librarians handed Jo a sleeping mat. She slept sandwiched between the shelves and tried not to picture books falling on her while she slept.

"Heavens, did you fall into the river, Ezra? You're leaving sinkholes in my nice carpet. Stand on the tile, go on."

"You don't need to shove me, grandpa." It was hard to miss the snap of Ezra's voice. "And why didn't you tell me the windmill was missing a whole wing-thing? No wonder the power sucks here. The radio's gonna be useless without it."

Jo held her breath so she could eavesdrop, peeking between the books to see shapes moving beyond them.

"Then fix it," Norman said mildly. "Isn't that why you've been pestering us so much?"

A sound of defeat floated into Jo's sleeping spot.

"What about your friend?" Norman asked. Jo's ears burned. "She's been lifting boxes twice her size today. If you need some muscle, I'm sure she-"

"She was just along for the ride," Ezra replied.
There were soft plunking sounds as Ezra and Norman pushed crates full of wire and metal rods along the carpet.

"I didn't mean to drop her on you. I'm sure she'll move along."

"She's not in my hair," Norman said. "You two having a spat or something?"

"No," said Ezra. "We're not—there's nothing to spat about. She barely says a word."

Norman hmmed.

"And I'm sure you gave her space to share her piece."
"What's that supposed to mean?" Ezra said. "She doesn't talk."

"She talked to me today."

Jo held her breath in case they could hear it.

"What? When? How?" Ezra demanded.

"Asked about her pop," Norman said. "She smiled when I told her that library story."

Jo focused on the floor and breathed until the bad images loosened their grip. She knew this feeling well. When her throat closed like that, there was no use forcing sound through it. Silence was easier, and didn't betray her.

Still, she felt moved to say *something*, and the feeling gnawed at her until the early hours of the morning when she decided she wouldn't rest easy until she talked to him.

Jo returned her sleeping mat to the librarian on duty while it was still dark outside, and she went out to look for Ezra. She inhaled the thick scent of rain, grass, wood, a tinge of rot. A cold drop of rain slid down her back.

The rain pelted along the rim of her hood as she squinted through the haze of morning and sniffed again. The sour note of decomposition made her nose hairs stand on end. There was a sound she couldn't place through the roll of thunder, like someone was dragging a heavy sack full of jelly along the earth.

"*CRAPCRAPCRAPCRAP!*" came a distant cry.

Jo picked up the pace, slipping once on the grass until she crested the hill to see Ezra, arms shaking as they propped up a metal grate three times his height. The grate was attached to a pulley system, but seemed to have slipped, leaving Ezra pinned under its weight. His glasses were fogged over with dew so Jo couldn't see his expression except by the way his jaw gawked open in terror.

The biter looked like a mound of moss slogging towards them, and Jo had the thought that she'd never seen one of those things grow so tall. Its skull stretched oddly towards the sky, bone sticking out at all angles to give it the appearance of wearing a jagged crown wrapped in coils of flowers. Jo placed the source of the strange sound: its long, mossy arms dragged on the ground, ripping two gaping rows in the earth as it passed.

Ezra made a noise like a deflating set of bagpipes, still bracing the fallen beam with two hands.

Jo leapt forward and she snatched the pulley ropes out of the air. Her palms stung against the spiny cable. She grit her teeth and heaved with Ezra once, twice, three times before they were able to lift it off of him. It crashed beside his head.

"What the *hell* is that thing?" Ezra wheezed, brushing himself off and picking up his fallen tools: he stashed a heavy wrench into his belt, though Jo knew it wouldn't come in handy against a biter whose head towered so high off the ground.

The creature gave a sluggish lurch in his direction. And then, to Jo's utter shock, the earth tore open and the creature's long, dragging arm came into view. If it hadn't been attached to the biter, Jo would have thought it was the long root of an oak tree.

The biter, still a great distance away, let out an eerie creaking sound like a trunk bending in the wind. Its arm ripped out of the ground, showering them with dirt.

"Uh," Ezra said dumbly.

Then, he disappeared from Jo's line of vision entirely. The biter's long arm was curled around his ankle like a python, and it yanked him so he faceplanted into the grass.

Jo unsheathed her knife and sliced at the thing's long arm, but it was thick and too fibrous for her blade. She started to saw through, which was a challenge because she had a wiggling Ezra on her left and a biter closing in, long arm pinning him in place as it slogged closer. With her other hand she fumbled for her firearm.

Biters were supposed to slow with time, rot back into the ground. This one hadn't. It kept growing, dragging the earth with it.

Still, she had to do *something.*

While Ezra dug his fingernails into the grass and the biter dragged him closer, Jo unloaded a few shots into the biter's head. It hardly slowed. Was there too much fiber in the way? Did its brain exist anymore?

Ezra was still shouting things, and Jo turned back in for a moment to hear him cry, *"Ax!"*

She ran into the shed, blood pumping hot while rain soaked cold into her skin. She tore through stacks of tools and ended up with a flat-edged shovel. She exploded back outside and raised the shovel over her head. Like a mad gardener, Jo cut Ezra's feet free.

The biter's arm curled up like a dead snake on the ground, but the biter, undeterred, still sludged towards them.

Ezra scrambled back to his feet, adjusted his glasses, and said in one breath,

"Right, okay. Jo, grab the pulley again—I couldn't pull the grate up on my own, but you did it so easily so I have no doubt—and wait for my signal."

Jo grabbed the rope once more and felt splinters puncture her palm. The biter was coming ever closer.

"Ready?" Ezra breathed. He was bleeding from both ankles from where the rope had sliced him up. He flashed her a thumbs-up and took off in the direction of the creature.

Despite the utter insanity of his action, Jo stayed put, arms quivering against the weight of the metal grate dangling on the other end. She could only wait and pray that someone from Roslyn was watching their absurd display and was coming to help.

Ezra pushed his foggy glasses up higher, raised his wrench, and gave it a little shake so it clinked.

"Yoohoo!" He sang. "Over heeeeeere!"

Flabbergasted, Jo looked on as the biter took another step towards him, maw hanging open. There was a dark cavern where the mouth had rotted away, and remnants of teeth glinted like stones in a riverbed. The earth moved again, and Ezra stiffened as he anticipated arm number two to rip out of the dirt and ensnare him again.

"LET GO!" He bellowed, and Jo did just that. Ezra leapt aside as the grate came crashing down onto the crown of the biter. The creature moaned and fell hard into the earth, pinned by metal bars.

"The head!" Said Ezra, looking as though he hadn't expected the plan to work. "Quick, the ground's doing that thing again—"

Jo ran up to the crash site with her shovel brandished over her head. She brought it down, slicing its jaw from its dodder crown. After a minute of hacking the thick growth of vines, Jo cleared a spot of skull, took aim with her firearm, and pulled the trigger. The rumble under the ground stopped, and there was no sound except the pattering of rain and distant shouts of approaching townspeople.

Ezra stepped back, wiping sopping wet bangs out of his eyes.

"Oh, *now* they show up," he said.

The two stood in the rain for a minute, gazing down at the overgrown biter and avoiding eye contact. Jo wiped her scraped hands on her pants as Ezra checked himself for other wounds besides his raw ankles.

Unable to stand the quiet, Ezra cleared his throat.

"You ever see one of 'em get this big? Because I haven't. Like, this isn't a person, this thing's a whole *ent,* right? *Lord of the Rings?*"

He wiped his glasses on his equally wet shirt.

"I, uh, saw you looking through that one the other day, so I…"

"Ezra," Jo said, halting him.

His eyes popped out, and if Jo wasn't so anxious about the crackliness of her voice, she might have laughed.

"Uh!" Ezra said. "Oh—sorry, that was rude. I just…never heard you actually talk before. And that's because I've been an idiot, talking over you so much."

He stopped himself.

"And I did it again. Agh. Sorry. You were saying?"

Jo swallowed.

"I'm s-sorry for the b-biter th-thing," she said deliberately, not looking at him. Her stutter would just be there and he could like it or not. "I d-didn't m-mean…"

Ezra shifted from foot to foot, his shoes making gentle slaps in the puddles at his feet.

"I thought I'd done something to piss you off," Ezra said quietly. "And I hated that."

Jo was glad for the rain. It offered another rhythm she could focus on as opposed to the silence.

"I just c-can't t-talk sometimes," she said and forced herself to make eye contact. Actually, Ezra's gaze was quite soft, and not like staring into a sun.

"It's like I…shut off. S-sometimes it's easier to just…listen."

She didn't have a better explanation, and mercifully, Ezra didn't ask for one.

"I didn't mean to push you," he said. "I'm a lot. I *know* I'm a lot. It's a disease. When I'm nervous, I just go off and I can't shut up. I take off. No stopping me."

His shoulders rose and fell.

"But it doesn't mean I don't care, or that I'm trying to…drown you out or not listen to you. I'm just not good with quiet. It makes me crazy. I can't turn my brain off. Guess we're wired different."

Jo nodded.

"Uh, yeah, so, thanks," he continued. "For that. For coming up here and…and saving my life and everything."

The rain pittered on the long, metal spokes of the radio antennae until a small crowd of people came up the hill with their weapons clutched in their hands.

"We're alive!" Ezra shouted. And then, in an undertone, "No thanks to you guys."

As the people of Roslyn approached to check on the two and gawk at the forest creature dead on the ground, Jo nudged Ezra and gestured to the grate, still attached to the tethers. "Want h-help?"

Ezra exhaled. "That would save me, I think."

Jo stayed to help him finish the tower. They worked wordlessly, hands numb, rain soaking through their clothes. When Ezra laughed, the sound surprised her. She realized she felt warm anyway.

17: LIBRARY

Jo helped Ezra with the tower for the rest of their time in Roslyn. He seemed happy to explain how the technical side of radio worked and was even more happy to show her how he charged solar batteries and ran wires underground. Jo could barely catch his lingo and the rate at which he talked, but it was still interesting to listen to.

And the library. Jo didn't know where to begin.

In her evenings wandering the large multi-floored building, she drank in every title of every book spine, things like *When We Were Birds* and *Little Women.* She'd pick up a few at a time and read hungrily whenever she and Ezra took a break in the shade. She devoured fiction, but the books on flora intrigued her, too. Burning Well tended gardens for a modest supply of vegetables, mostly potatoes and roots. But Jo loved looking at the sketches of the earth, the layers of soil, how roots crawled down deep while the green bits sprouted up.

The librarians didn't ask for anything when a stranger needed a place to hide, or needed information, or when they just needed to read a schlocky crime novel and escape reality in some purple prose.

One of the strangest arrivals was a small group of teenagers who looked like they'd raided an abandoned costume shop. They wore cloaks straight from *Dracula,* triangle hats with feathers, and backpacks stuffed with fabrics Jo had never seen in the wild: glitter, sequins, animal print, neon feathers. They clustered at the front desk, expectant.

"Shakespeare section, I take it?" Norman said dryly, jerking his head toward the stairs. "You put everything back exactly where you found it. I don't wanna be cleaning up after you all again."

"Got extra paper, Normie?" The girl in the front asked, leaning far over the desk so Norman shooed her back. "We need to make a couple more copies. We're adding some people to the cast."

"To *Macbeth?*" Norman said, and the group shushed him.

"Dare'st he speak the forbidden name?" said one. *"Thou sodden-ridden lord!"*

Norman did not crack a smile.

"That superstition only applies when you're *inside* a theater."

"Well, we're not doing that one anymore, anyway," one of the boys said dismissively.

"Again?" Norman sneered. "I'll be shocked if you have anything to present at this rate. What is it? I should hope it's something a bit more comedic, considering the current state of things."

He adjusted his specs.

"Much Ado About Nothing? A Midsummer Night's Dream? That one was a crowd-pleaser back in my day."

"What are you talking about? *Mackers* is hilarious," said Zoe, and turned to one of her fellow actresses to proclaim, *"Is this a dagger which I see before me, the handle toward my hand? Come, let me clutch thee."*

The troupe cackled.

"Jo," said Norman, pinching his temples, "would you grab the clown dropouts some paper so I don't have to speak to them?"

The troupe galumphed behind Jo as she led them to one of the shelves and pulled down a heavy box of paper.

"New librarian, huh?" Zoe said with a bright smile.

Jo shook her head.

"Just h-helping out."

"Do you mind grabbing *Twelfth Night,* too? We gotta copy our lines."

Twelfth Night? How did she not realize? Jo blinked, shocked for a few seconds.

"Th-they have that h-here?" she said.

"Yeah. I've seen a bunch of copies." Zoe squinted her round eyes. "Something the matter?"

Jo was sure she had stopped breathing.

Twelfth Night, the play she'd always regretted not reading—Ruth's play—was right here in the library.

The Suncrest Players were gathered in the study room for the rest of the day and most of the next one. As Jo went back and forth helping Norman inside and then Ezra outside—she was glad to keep busy—she caught snippets of what the Suncrest kids were reading in loud whispers.

"Speak your office."

"It alone concerns your ear. I bring no overture of war, no taxation of homage—"

"It's *homage.* You don't pronounce the 'h,' Zoe," said one of the boys. He had dark skin and jet-black hair swept in a low ponytail.

"Well, I don't know. I've only ever read this word."

"We should just ask Norman. Didn't he used to direct?"

"No way. I don't want that know-it-all telling us how to Shakespeare. *I hold the olive in my hand. My words are as full of peace as matter...*"

"Norman!" called the boy to a chorus of shushing. "Could you see what we've got so far?"

Zoe looked sour as Norman hunched over, and Jo had the suspicion he'd been listening to them rehearse with rapt attention.

"For starters," Norman said, "you're all forgetting your iambic pentameter."

"We're just learning lines," Zoe mumbled.

"I can explain it again if you like."

"No, thanks," said Zoe.

"If you mark out your beats properly," Norman went on briskly, "and add a little rhythm to each line: *In sooth, I know not why I am so sad.*' There, do you see how I'm emphasizing every other word like that?"

Jo couldn't guess what an iambic pentameter was, but whatever it was, it was making Zoe seethe.

"He's just trying to help," muttered one of the girls when Norman strolled off to help a new visitor.

"He's probably been itching to do something theatre-related for a decade."

"Well, then he should go do his own play," Zoe said, marking her handwritten script with an extra sharp gesture. "It's hard enough trying to put something together without some pompous old-world director telling me I'm doing it wrong. People just want to feel normal for a second. They want to see a show, and they don't care if it's perfect or not."

There was scattered consent, and Jo found it strange how the work of one dead man could still start a fight.

Once the players finished copying their lines, Jo took *Twelfth Night* back and read it cover to cover. She couldn't bring it outside the library, but Norman allowed her to hold onto it while she slept there. She read through the whole paperback every night.

From the hilltop where the tower was underway, Jo and Ezra could see the people bustling around Roslyn, and fire smoke rising into a blue sky. The Roslyn windmill creaked above their heads, sun-dappled and still. She watched the small acting troupe exit the gates, no doubt on their way back to Suncrest, their backpacks bulging with handwritten Shakespeare.

"Have you heard anything about Rafael?" Ezra asked, chucking her an apple he'd snagged from the kitchens. He was sitting cross-legged in the grass, chewing noisily as he fiddled with the wires on his radio box. "Has anyone seen him?"

Jo shook her head despondently and continued to hammer the broken windmill wing she was tasked to fix.

"That sucks," Ezra said. "But people come in and out of Roslyn all the time. I'm sure news will pop up eventually."

He sucked his teeth as he twisted a new copper wire into the back of the casing. "We'll be done with the tower soon, and I'm moving on to the next town over. I know Norm can use you in the library, that is, if you want to hang back here and wait for your pop."

Jo hammered in the final nail in the wing.

"I don't know," she said honestly.

Ezra said nothing for a minute, only continued to fiddle with his radio box.

"Well," he said at last. "With the radio working, we can call each other anytime. You can catch me up on all the hot Roslyn gossip. I know you love to gab."

"Hm," she said, almost smiling. "M-maybe he passed through Suncrest."

"You never know," Ezra said, looking considerably more cheerful as he gave his electrical tape a tear with his teeth. "We can stick to the original plan and put word out via radio. Plus, we really can't miss a Suncrest production of *Twelfth Night,* can we?"

Helping Ezra with the radio tower gave her something to do with her hands, and that felt close enough to safe.

"Are you sure it's r-ready?" Jo asked, looking at the headset Ezra was wrapping generously in electrical tape. She'd done what she could to fix the windmill, but even though the task had left her sore in muscles she didn't know she had, she wasn't sure it caught the wind well enough with its gimpy wing.

"I think it'll generate enough to call old Theo," said Ezra, turning a dial on the dashboard. "My brother. You met him?"

Jo had barely held her head up enough to meet many people back in Ambridge. "D-don't think so."

"It's okay. He's a prick, anyway."

Before the test run, Ezra spent their final day stapling thick strips of fabric and foam on the comm center walls to soundproof them. Jo helped him secure cables while he hovered around, triple-checking the connection to the tower.

"So far, so good," Ezra mumbled and fiddled with the knobs on his box some more. "Wanna listen?"

Jo brought her ear close to his headset. There was a sound like static buzzing there. She grinned at him.

Their work had actually done something.

Ezra stuck his tongue out. "Now, if I just tune it to the right…" Then he practically fell off his stool. Jo had heard it, too.

There was a voice. Someone was talking in the headphones.

"…c…come in…Roslyn? Th…you?…is Ambri…helloooo over there?"

"Yeah! Hello! Hi! I mean, wait–" Ezra flailed about for a minute, unplugging the headphones and trading them for the radio's speakers. Then he snatched up the microphone and said, "Prophet here, coming at you all the way from Roslyn! How's it sound, buddy-boy? Over."

"Ehhh…muddy. But you're not breaking up too much. That's good. Over."

Ezra pumped the air with his fist. "Yes! Holy crap, it works! You can really hear me and everything? Over?"

"Yeah, so you really don't have to shout into the mic for me to hear you, dude. Over."

Ezra did a little dance around the floor.

"Okay! Success! Right, Jo? I mean—sorry, code names, code names. What d'you wanna be? I guess we should have talked about that before we went on the air, as it were, but—"

"Hey, we're not still doing those, are we? Judee doesn't do them so we've just been saying our own on the walkies. Over."

"You never know who might be listening!" Ezra said delightedly. "So you better get used to it, Gilmore! Over!"

His grin was infectious, and Jo had to admit that it was pretty cool to see the results of weeks of hard work. She listened to the gravelly feedback while Ezra asked about how Ambridge was faring and if there was any news or gossip.

"Biters were coming in hordes a few days ago. We think something scared them down the hill. No one got bit, though. And no one's crossed our borders, not that we've seen," said Theo, to which Jo sank a little. *"I know your partner was looking for her pop. Sorry. Over."*

"Thank y-you," Jo said, and there was a pause on the other end.

"Bro, I think the connection's weird, your voice sounded–"

"No, no, that's her. Over."

"Oh. Hello. Over."

"Hello," said Jo. Ezra nudged her. "Um. O-over."

"I thought you weren't a talker. Over."

"I'm n-not," said Jo. "O-over."

There was static, and Theo's chuckle floated through.

"Well, I'm glad someone was there to do the heavy lifting. Over."

"My partner here—code name TBD—was the muscle, granted, but I was the brains. Over," said Ezra.

"Aww, cute," said Theo, and Ezra turned slightly pink.

When Jo and Ezra traveled back down the hill towards town, they stopped at the base of the radio tower to look up at their handiwork. The tower held unbendingly against the breeze, and every memory she had of tightening bolts, welding the metal, and securing that gold Ezra-flag were as clear as water in her mind.

"It's good, huh?" Ezra said, his bravado softening as she beamed at him. "You up for one more?"

As they packed their things for Suncrest, Jo found herself feeling a twang of sentimentality over leaving the quiet refuge of the library. Handling the worn books, devouring the stories by lantern light, even listening to Ezra read sections of stories when they took breaks from construction, it all was a brief respite from the grim outside. Even Norman gave her a kind of soft look when she went to drop *Twelfth Night* onto his desk.

"Would you like to take a copy of this?" Norman asked her. She raised her eyebrows questioningly.

"Volunteers make handwritten copies for anyone to take out," he explained. "We have an overabundance of Shakespeare, and I would certainly recommend becoming well acquainted with his original work before seeing the, well, *creative* version our Suncrest Players are undoubtedly planning on doing."

Jo thanked Norman with a firm, grateful handshake. She made room in her backpack to shove the 120-page bound notes between her rations and socks. Her shoulders ached with the weight, but she didn't care.

As she went up the winding staircase to find Ezra, Norman greeted the two travelers who had just walked in through the oak doors— they looked awed by the place.

"New here, huh?" Norman asked them. "Make sure you read the rules before you venture too deep."

"We love what y'all do here. Always wanted to see inside."

There was something so familiar about that low drawl, and for a moment Jo thought she could be wrong.

But then, as she peered over the edge of the banister, the glimmer of hope drained out of her.

A Wolfskin leaned against the front desk. His coat was unfastened, rifle slung loose at his back, a pale scar cutting down the side of his neck. Jo didn't recognize his face, but she recognized the build, the jacket, the cropped hair.

"...partner and I are just passin' through," the Wolfskin said easily. "Ya'll got anything on fishin'? Think I could use a few pointers. Maybe a place to sit for a while."

"Guidebooks are up the stairs on the right," Norman replied. "Where you folks comin' from, anyhow?"

"Up North," the other one replied. Tom, by the sound of his voice. "Had to get away from all the fighting."

Norman whistled through his teeth.

"What with Burning Well people slinking around, and now Redgrass knocking on our door offering 'protection.' With their uniforms, all smiles. Pheh. Evil is what it is."

"Horrible," Tom said, his voice slick and sympathetic.

Jo shuddered.

"You all feel safe in here? Is this place well protected?"

"Absolutely. We've got some well-trained people looking out. I figure as long as we keep our heads down, the Northerners will wear each other out."

Norman sent the Wolfskins up the stairs, right past Jo's hiding spot. Keeping behind the rows of shelves, Jo quietly crept after them. She caught glimpses of their coat sleeves through the spaces between books. Boots stopped in front of her shelf, and Jo ducked down.

"This is a big place," Tom hissed, pretending to thumb through the volumes. "What do you think?"

"All the towns we've passed through say they're protected," the Wolfskin murmured, flipping idly through a book on fishing lures.

"They always are, right up until they're not. You think Sienna and the others bumped into any…any trouble?" Tom continued.

"You mean the captain's stray?" the Wolfskin said. "If she's still breathing, she's keeping low. But someone always finds them."

"No, not her. I'm talkin' about Redgrass."

"If anyone can convince them to join us, it's Sienna."

"I dunno." Tom craned his head around, and Jo sunk lower into the carpet. "It don't feel right fighting in a library."

Jo strained to listen for a few more minutes, but their voices had dropped in volume and she was unable to pick anything more out. Nothing more about Sienna or Nell, and not a whisper of Rafael.

Every nerve in Jo's body screamed to flee, but she forced herself to wait for the two to slip back down the staircase.

There were Wolfskins in Roslyn, and they were *looking*.

Jo sat with her back to the far corner of the comms center, feet ready to spring at the first sight of Wolfskins poking their noses through the door.

It felt like hours when Ezra finally slipped back into the radio shed and locked the door behind him. He drew the ragged curtains back an inch to peek through.

"Norman's telling the other librarians what's up," Ezra said breathlessly. "They clocked the insignia on the coats. Same ones we've been hearing about."

Ezra flipped the curtain closed.

"We can leave out the side gate. Norman will radio ahead to Suncrest and tell 'em to look out for us. Man. It's a good thing we got it working, huh?"

Logically, it was not her fault that the Wolfskins had targeted Roslyn.

"A dog'll hunt," Rafael used to say.

But the guilt lingered. The smell of smoke clung to her nose.

Jo and Ezra waited until the sun touched the mountains, and then they followed Norman's instructions and snuck along the Roslyn wall, out the gate, and back into the unfamiliar woods. Ezra led them to a line of train tracks, and they followed that until the moon rose high and bright as silver in the sky. They jumped at every sound, and even the occasional moan of biters weaving through the trees was a small comfort. Biters over Wolfskins.

They walked all night, and at noon the next day searched for a hidden place to bunker down. Jo rested her eyes but did not sleep. Her ears were peeled for any sound of a boot step disturbing the forest floor. She hoped that Norman was okay. She hoped it was true that no one messed with the library.

After only three hours of no sleep, they veered away from the railroad tracks and dipped further into the forest. There was a packed path that Ezra kept in sight, and through the fingers of the tangled brush, Jo could make out an old playground made of wood. It was sprouting ivy like the ground was swallowing it up. The old swings dangled on the ground, creaking with rust with every shift in the breeze. The whole thing stood like a dying, wooden giant.

As soon as they stepped into the clearing, Jo knew it was a fatal mistake. A twig snapped, and then like a freight train, pressure crashed into her back, knocking the air out of her lungs. Pain shot like tiny arrows through her ribs. She reached for her weapon, but a thick hand grasped her wrist until she thought the bone would break. Their eyes were hidden behind two black pools of a gas mask.

Somewhere to her left, Jo could see a red tangle as Ezra writhed against someone twice his size. Jo tore up the earth with her feet, but her cries were stifled by a mouthful of dirt and a knee in her diaphragm.

Somewhere in the chaos, she heard Ezra say her name, a crack like thunder, and then, a silent nothing.

18: REDGRASS

Jo saw the sky through the slats in the roof. Dusk. A spattering of stars. She let her eyelids droop heavily. For a few small seconds, she was floating. But the rigid edges of a chair dug into the base of her neck.

The smell of mildew on wood. A tinge of gun smoke. Ezra nowhere.

With great effort, Jo raised her head, blinking rapidly as the small storeroom came into focus. She was in a straight-backed chair. She was untied. The gas masks Jo saw in the clearing dangled from a hook on the far wall. There were no windows, only two people staring at her, decked in camouflage brown.

The woman's mouth curved. "You're Rafael's girl."

Jo recognized the brand poking out from under her shaved hair: four vertical stripes embedded red and angry in her scalloped skin. It was the Redgrass brand.

Jo swallowed.

"Sienna said he turned." The woman leaned her weight onto one hip. "Turned on your people. Traitor, is what she called him."

Jo's throat ached.

"Th-that's n-not—"

"We didn't ask what you think," the man cut in. "We asked where he ran."

"If he's dead," the woman said, "that's Burning Well's mess. If he's alive…"

She shrugged.

"Then he's Sienna's problem."

The man stepped closer.

"You should be grateful we didn't kill you outright. Burning Well asked us to. Said you were loose ends."

Jo's stomach dropped.

"But," the woman continued, "we don't like being told what to do. And we like knowing things."

Her gaze slid over Jo, slow and assessing.

"So for now, you stay."

"For now," the man echoed.

The muddied pool of Jo's mind cleared, and she whipped her head around the sparse room.

"E-Ezra?" she rasped. She half-expected his lopsided grin to grace her from somewhere behind the strangers, but her companion was nowhere to be found. Her stomach lurched. The last thing she recalled was him disappearing behind the hill, his strangled cry ringing in her ears.

"Your friend? Sorry," said the man, not sounding an ounce sorry. "We didn't recognize him, so I left him in the woods somewhere."

Jo stood up that time, her eyes blazing, and had to brace herself on the chair. The room spun.

"Where is h-he?" she said.

"Look, kid, you tell us what we need to know, then we'll show you where we left his body. How's that?"

Jo grit her jaw so her teeth ground. Ezra couldn't have been gone. Jo just saw him. It was senseless. He had one more tower to build. It wasn't fair.

"We're not sending you back to Burning Well," the woman said. "And we're not killing you either."

The man snorted.

"Yet."

She ignored him.

"You'll sit. You'll listen. And if Burning Well comes sniffing around asking questions?" Her eyes flicked to Jo's ribs. "We'll decide what you're worth then. Burning Well doesn't give orders unless they expect payment."

The Redgrassers closed in like prongs of a pitchfork. Two sets of strong arms clamped on her biceps, pinning them painfully behind. The woman was gripping the curved handle of Jo's hunting knife and held it up in the last beams of the dipping sun.

Jo cried out as they struck her spine. The blade of her own knife appeared at her nose. The woman's stern gaze bored into Jo's eyes as if the answers were there somewhere.

"Where's Rafael hiding, hm? Or where'd you last see him?"

A hot sting as the blade bit Jo's cheek.

"Don't you be shy now, girlie."

"She's not saying anything."

"Should I carve that tongue out? You don't seem to like to use it."

"We need her alive. If Rafael's still in play—"

Jo wrenched her jaw open.

"D-d-don't…"

"Stuttering baby," said the woman. "Don't what? Don't drive this into your kneecap?"

"DON'T. KNOW," Jo said.

"Don't know what?"

She wanted to know where he was. She needed to know where Rafael was.

"Don't know. Don't know. Don't know. Don't know. Don't—"

"Enough of this," the man grunted.

Jo flinched as he grinned at her with his yellowing teeth, and true fear coursed through her body like venom.

Ezra saw the long, white stretches of cloud dragging along a sea of sky. The grass poked into the nape of his neck, his vision spun dreamily.

After a minute, the ringing in his ears eased. Birdsong. Something hot and sticky on his brow. The sky stopped turning. His head throbbed.

Then, a strange cry. An animal?

It sounded again, high and wrenching. Ezra lifted his head and—

"Jo!" he shouted, without thinking.

The sound echoed back in the trees.

The brush ahead shuddered. Ezra scrambled backward, palm brushing once against a thin wire frame. His glasses had skidded off his face and vanished into the grass. He shoved them back onto his nose and then the smell hit him—something sweet gone bad.

Biters.

They emerged in ones and twos at first, shapes peeling away from the green. They stood still in the long fingers of the sun, and Ezra would not have seen them unless he had stopped.

"Great," he whispered. "Great, great, good, great, GREAT."

One stepped forward with an odd, jerky gait. Then another. Then three more grew interested, their decaying mouths opening as they turned toward him. It was always a surprise to see their mossy limbs move so quickly.

Ezra leaped back, feet sinking into thick patches of flowers. He made to run when a skeletal hand tangled itself in the laces of his boot and yanked him down.

"No…you…don't," he breathed, panic rising like water in his lungs as more hands went grasping for his jacket.

With a high-pitched scream that would have been embarrassing had he not been fighting for his life, Ezra kicked free, slipped out of his boot, slid once on his sock, and booked it back the way he'd come.

He didn't stop until his chest burned. When he finally did, he bent double and feverishly checked his arms, his neck, his legs.

The only thing he found was a scratch on his brow, sticky and hot, from his initial fall. No bites.

A drop of relief.

Ezra wiped his face with his sleeve and straightened. His backpack was not where he'd dropped it. He hadn't really expected it to be, but dismay crept in at the thought of strangers rifling through his blueprints and tools. If he was going to put up another tower in Suncrest, he would need his blowtorch. His special wrench.

And Jo—

He swallowed.

Jo was not where he'd left her. Which was another level of—well, Ezra wasn't even sure if they were technically friends. But she was his travel companion, at the very least. She'd saved his life more than once.

He scanned the ground for something familiar. A shoelace. A hair clip—though she didn't wear those, did she? Her hair was shaved close. The dirt held only a churn of footprints.

Ezra wiped his glasses on his shirt, set them back on his cut nose, and followed the tracks, keeping to the trees. Through the oaks, thin pillars of smoke threaded upward. A camp. He swallowed and slipped deeper into the shade.

She had just started talking to him. And, well, he needed the extra set of hands on the towers. More importantly, he hadn't found her body. That had to count for something positive.

The hope didn't last.

Even through smeared lenses, Ezra could make out a small caravan moving toward the smoke. Gas masks. One of them carried a long, bundled shape over his shoulder.

Jo.

"You're an idiot," Ezra told himself, and followed at a distance.

He wouldn't have found the sewer grate if he hadn't been without a shoe. Cold mire seeped through his sock, and his heel struck metal. He scraped away mud and stared at a rusted latch set into the ground.

Untouched, mostly. Which meant nothing.

Traveling unseen beat wandering the woods. Ezra chose the tunnel.

"You're an idiot," he said again, but the words dissolved under the memory of Jo's animal cry. Friends? Maybe not. Not yet.

It took ten minutes for Ezra to pry the grate loose. When it finally gave, he swung his legs over the edge and dropped inside.

The sewer ceiling scraped his scalp as he hunched forward. Every step, he waited to be seen, or shot. To have his brains painted along the wall.

"You're good, Ez," he murmured. "Everything's fine. Peachy. Just you. Just the walls and the water. Maybe don't look too close at the water. Yeah. That's better."

He kept moving, alone in the dark.

He walked, comforting himself with his low murmuring, breathing the stale and sour air, and trying not to feel faint. His one shoeless foot felt frozen as it splashed through the trickle of questionable, brown liquid. If Ezra didn't contract gangrene by the end of the trek, that would certainly be a bonus.

And if he was alive by the end, well, that would be a miracle.

He had half a mind to circle back to Roslyn. There, he could get help, hell, another shoe. But the walk back would take too long, if he wasn't mauled by biters by the end of the journey, and by then Jo could be...

Pale moonlight trickled in from a grate above his head, and Ezra jumped as he caught sight of a pair of eyes. Someone was standing above the grate, smoking, the tip of her rolled cigarette glowing. She took a long drag and blew the smoke so it curled. Her eyes averted lazily.

Ezra slipped out of the line of light. She hadn't seen him.

Honestly, he was surprised he'd lived so long in the current days with his eyesight as bad as it was. Theo always joked that as soon as Ezra broke his glasses, he was a dead man. Not such a funny thing to joke about, now that he was right in the beating heart of danger. He waited for the guard's smoke to disappear, and for her footsteps to fade before he set off again.

Ezra came upon a ladder and stopped. What was the plan? Find Jo? Find his backpack? Was it stupid to wander around and pretend to be a lost new recruit?

Maybe it was because he'd have done anything to breathe the air again, or maybe he was feeling extra stupid and reckless. Whatever it was, he gripped the slimy ladder rungs, whispered one last "well" before rising carefully through the grate.

He ducked behind the first structure he saw, anticipating a bullet between his eyes. None came. He took inventory of his surroundings: a few low sheds, an open yard churned to mud, watchers up on the wall, breathing out sour smoke.

He pressed his back to the wood and waited until his pulse slowed enough to think.

He was good at sticking his nose in places it didn't belong, as Judee always liked to remind him. All he had to do was poke around for Jo without getting caught.

A cough carried across the yard and Ezra froze in place.

One of the guards crossed the open ground with something slung over his shoulder. Ezra's stomach lurched as the frayed, canvas shape came into focus.

It was his backpack.

He kicked open the door to a narrow shed and tossed the pack inside like trash. The door swung shut, a loose latch falling into place.

Seething, Ezra waited for the guard to wander back toward the fire barrel. Then he crossed the yard hunched low, timing his steps with the creak of the wall and the mutter of voices. At the shed, he tried the latch. It rattled but held, which he should have expected.

So he slid his fingers along the warped wood until he found a split near the hinge and worked it wider, just enough to slip his hand through.

He said a thank-you as the door gave with a soft crack.

Ezra pulled the door closed behind him and dropped to a knee, hands shaking as he dug through the mess.

His pack was there, all ripped open and his tools spilling out of it. His blueprints were bent and smudged with dirt, but otherwise untouched.

"Neanderthals," he uttered, scooping his belongings back into the bag and listening for noise outside.

His heart was knocking against his ribs like it wanted out. He reached under the central worktable for his wrench, fingers brushing cold metal, when he noticed what was spread across the surface.

A map, the corners held down by a few stones. It was a map of the valley.

His stomach dipped as he read the names scrawled in the margins, each one circled hard enough to tear the paper: *Roslyn. Suncrest. Ambridge.*

Kettering, crossed out.

Arrows bled outward from a single point at the center: *BW.*

Ezra followed the notes scribbled blotchily along the edges, like someone didn't want to waste time: *Numbers light. After harvest. Redgrass support pending.*

And one name, written larger than the rest, pressed so hard it had dented the paper beneath it: *C. Rafael*

Next to it, in different ink, tight and controlled: *Spotted.*

Below that, underlined once: *Alive.*

Ezra let out a shaky breath that almost turned into a laugh.

Alive.

A noise from outside snapped him back into himself. Ezra ducked lower, and noticed a small ledger poking out from underneath the maps. He flipped it open and noted the little dates at the top and a scattering of notes on each day. Patrol sightings, a delivery, a hostage, an execution – "Yeesh" – biters, another delivery…

He flipped to the latest entry and there, written small as an afterthought: *BW girl - holding*

There was no name, but Ezra didn't need one.

In a rush of reckless certainty, he swept the map and the ledger together and crammed them into his bag. They tore, but he didn't care.

A hand brushed the door outside. Ezra clapped a hand over his mouth.

The door rattled once. Ezra closed his eyes. A voice came, and the rattling stopped.

Footsteps moved on.

Ezra stayed there just long enough to get his breathing under control. His eyes snagged on a hook by the door—two gas masks hanging there, black lenses clouded with old breath. He hesitated only a second before grabbing one and tugging it down over his face. The elastic pinched his temple and the smell inside was sour and lived-in.

Perfect.

Then he slung the bag over his shoulder, eased the door open a fraction, and slipped back into the dark.

"I'm coming, Jo," he whispered, the words barely sound at all.

Jo pulled her knees up to her chin, careful to grip the parts of her flesh that had not been branded. The underground room was ice cold despite the hulking broiler across from her. Her limbs pulsed with dull pain.

Ezra.

The name landed heavy and useless. He talked too much. He tripped over his own feet. But he still had one more tower to build. It wasn't fair.

She closed her eyes, saw him slip on the wire rig and land hard on his ass, heard his indignant yelp. The memory surprised a weak chuckle out of her.

She couldn't stay here.

Her foggy gaze wandered to the crate sitting five feet beyond her bars, where the tools of her tormentors lay: long metal pokers and brands of various shapes and sinister lengths. And, folded neatly, there was her jacket. They may have let her keep her jeans and tee, but they wouldn't waste a good leather jacket like the one Rafael had given her.

She stretched her arm out, the bars chilling her skin. She was just about to try sticking her leg through when the basement's heavy door creaked open, and a hulking figure stepped inside. He noticed her poking through the bars and lunged forward.

His heavy hands closed around her wrists, and he yanked her violently against the cage. His horrible grin flashed like a warning light.

She spat in his eye.

In the split second of his flinch, Jo twisted his wrists down hard against the bars. The crack of his fingers rang against the bars. He swore and staggered back.

"You little—"

Pain exploded through her ribs as his boot drove through the bars and caught her square in the side. She hit the far wall hard, breath tearing out of her in a thin sound she didn't recognize as her own.

He straightened, furious now. Keys jangled at his belt.

"You're gonna pay for that," he said, and bent to the lock.

The door swung open, and Jo lunged for it.

He was on her in a second, his sausage-fingers closed around her throat. Stars burst behind her eyes, and the edges of the room went dark.

Then, his hands vanished. There was a thud.

"Jo."

Her name reached her like someone was saying it from another room.

"Jo—hey—hey, you're okay. You're okay." Her eyelids fluttered open. A pair of black lenses loomed over her.

"You're *alive,*" the voice said, breaking. "I thought…thank God, I thought—"

Jo pushed herself onto her elbows, daring to believe it.

"Ez…*Ezra?*"

He removed his headgear and grinned down at her, his dark curls sticking in every direction and his glasses askew. Jo had never been happier to see his disheveled, cut-riddled face.

"H-how did you f-find me?" she asked.

"These guys aren't half as clever as they think they are. Careful," Ezra replied smugly, helping her to her feet. "Listen, I found something else. But we can't stay here."

She glanced at the guard on the floor.

"Is he…?"

"He's down," Ezra said. His hands shook. "Didn't wanna use my gun, would've made too much noise. See? I'm not totally stupid. So I decided to bash him, and all I could find was this pipe."

Jo reclaimed her outer layers of clothing, which had fallen onto the floor in the tussle. She pulled her outer layer over her tee, then zipped up her jacket. She yanked her jeans up, wincing as the fabric brushed her wounds.

"We need to go," Ezra anxiously repeated. He replaced his gas mask and then pulled Jo's hood up over her head. "I started a fire out there, but I think it's spreading a lot faster than I'd anticipated. Distractions, right?"

Jo nearly choked.

"You s-started a what?"

"Well, there was no other way to get the guards away from the door," Ezra said, as though it was common sense. It wasn't what she would have done, personally, but if it was crazy enough to work, who was she to judge?

Ezra pulled her towards the exit and she followed him to a sewer grate. There was smoke clogging the air, which thinned as they dropped into the tunnels and broke into a run.

Flashes of orange appeared above Jo's head, brief glimpses through the grates of flames. They continued on, Ezra without hesitating, navigating the tunnels like he'd done them a hundred times.

When they at last climbed back into the night, three Redgrass guards stared back. Someone fired.

Ezra stumbled and went down hard.

Jo hit the ground beside him as the guards scattered into the dark, drawn by the roaring fire blooming up from Redgrass.

Ezra was drenched in blood. She patted his head, his shoulders, and his chest to find any point of entry. Ezra wiped his mouth with the back of one trembling hand.

"Y-you're okay. That's really good," he was babbling. "I-I'm not good. Not good."

Jo found a gunshot wound high on his thigh, the blood sticky through his jeans. She got to work wrapping the wound in a torn piece of her shirt. She'd helped Wolfskins dress such wounds before and knew that Ezra would need antibiotics for a wound so open, so deep.

Jo tore another piece and tied it off hard. Ezra cried out.

"Stay with me," she said.

As midnight settled over the valley, it brought the moaning of the woods. The buzz of a night bug. An owl.

The true pain hit Ezra a few hours later. His leg reddened, skin tight and angry, every step teeth-gritting agony. Jo hauled him as fast as she could manage. The thought of stopping was worse.

But when she carried him lower into the valley, she met a biter. She halted.

At least, she thought it was a biter.

Where a head should have been, a cluster of violet flowers bloomed, thick and heavy like a tied bouquet. Leaves wove the frame where muscle used to be. Anything human had been claimed and reshaped. It moved slowly, dreamlike, its long leafy arms dragging soundlessly across the forest floor.

In a moment, it would hear them and lunge. Jo calculated how quickly she could put Ezra down and reach for the gun.

"It's okay," Ezra murmured. "It won't do anything."

The creature stood soaking in moonlight, particles drifting around its flowered crown. It didn't seem to notice them at all.

That, or it did not care.

Jo eased Ezra down against a log and stayed crouched there, one hand braced on the ground.

The creature stood where it had been, flowered crown tilted toward the moon, leaves shuddering in the breeze. It did not acknowledge them.

Ezra shifted weakly.

"You should sit," he murmured. "It's okay."

She didn't like the idea. Resting in the open went against everything Rafael had drilled into her. But her vision pinched at the edges, and when she tried to stand, her knees locked. She tentatively sat.

"It's a bloomer," Ezra added, eyes half-lidded, like he was pointing out a type of butterfly.

As they rested, a low sound rose from deeper in the valley. Jo stiffened as shapes moved between the trunks, bodies dragging. A biter horde, close enough that she could hear the soft pull of their feet through the damp earth. She clamped the hilt of her knife as they came close, shuffling and moaning and…

…passed by.

They moved around the clearing in a wide, slow arc, not one of them turning their heads. They flowed past the bloomer like water around a stone.

Jo squeezed her eyes shut for one count, then two. When she opened them again, the woods were empty.

Only the bloomer remained, standing watchlessly nearby.

19: SUNCREST

Suncrest let them in because they recognized Ezra, and Jo didn't question it. She helped carry him through the gates and warned the sentries about Wolfskins and Redgrass scouts in the woods. The guards exchanged looks and moved faster after that.

The medics cleaned the wound, gave him antibiotics, and told her he would live, but nothing more. Jo camped beside his cot and watched him toss and turn, her ears open for any change in his breathing. Her dreams were full of blooming biters in the pale light of the moon.

In the morning, Ezra's hand dangled off the cot, his long fingers twitching slightly. Jo reached out, hesitated, then took his hand in hers. Ice cold. She thought she felt his fingers curl around hers.

She was extremely surprised to see Norman in Suncrest the next afternoon. He looked thin and travel-worn.

"I locked the library the moment they left," he said quietly. "If they come back, they'll find nothing but books and stubborn old men."

When she asked what he was doing in Suncrest, he looked baffled at the question.

"I came to see Shakespeare, of course," he said as though it was obvious. "Even before the outbreak I caught every show. Broadway, Off-Broadway, every dinner theatre and school play I could catch a train to. Ask the Players. I haven't missed one yet. And it's good for me to get out of that library once in a while."

Jo felt her jaw loosen.

"B-but Redgrass is out there, and the b-biters are…"

Norman waved his hand as if shooing flies.

"The world is always happening," he said. "So I might as well enjoy what may be my final play."

His eyes drifted to Ezra's cot where he snoozed.

"Do you know," he said, more gently, "there was a time when I called Ezra to hook up the library's lights? That boy fell right through the ceiling, and do you know what he did? He apologized to *me*. Not a bump on that thick head of his."

Norman placed a gnarled hand on her shoulder.

"He's made of strong stuff, my dear," he said. "And so are you."

The Suncrest Players managed to convince Jo to eat with them that evening, so she left Ezra's bedside to join them at the canteen, where they stood in line for ladles of stew.

Jo forced food down and listened to the Players talk about preparations for their upcoming show. They conversed about props and intermissions and clowns and how they wouldn't be memorized in time, no way.

There weren't many young people in Burning Well that Jo felt okay being around, besides Nell and some of the brides.

"You worked at the library, didn't you?" one of the kids asked, eyeing Jo.

"She doesn't work there. She's with Ez," Zoe said, spewing soup so the others ducked to dodge her spit. "Word on the street, she's a crack shot, huh, Jo? Ezra was telling me back in Roslyn how she took on a small horde of biters all on her own. Just one by one, slash, pow, dead."

Jo felt her face grow warm.

"Woah," said Andrés, mouth ajar. "How did you manage that? And you didn't even get a scratch?"

Zoe nudged Jo's shoulder.

"Apparently, she used Ezra as a distraction."

There was a pause and then raucous laughter. Jo couldn't help it. She grinned, too.

"Okay, but how'd you do it?" Andrés said, wiping a tear. "The biters? You didn't use guns or anything?"

"No, that's n-noisy," Jo mumbled. The group was still staring at her. So she went on slowly, "You get b-behind it. Then you b-break a knee."

"Wait, so…" Andrés yanked a giggling Zoe up to demonstrate. "Like this..?"

Jo demonstrated, careful not to actually touch her boot to Zoe's knee.

"They're brittle," Jo said plainly. "You h-hobble 'em. Harder to get you when they can't w-walk."

The group spent the rest of dinner practicing and rough-housing until they were told to quiet down. Jo and Zoe watched from a safe distance.

"Who taught you all that?" Zoe asked with a note of curious reverence. Jo wrapped her arms around her knees.

"My dad."

Zoe looked thoughtful.

"Ez mentioned that," she said. "He taught you how to survive out there, huh? Wish I'd gotten some of that before my mom…well."

She played with the choppy locks at the base of her neck.

"Ezra said you're looking for him. You think he could be out there?"

Jo shrugged and winced as her shirt brushed against the welts on her arms.

Even if Rafael was miraculously alive, Jo knew that nothing would ever be the same again. It couldn't be. Deep down, she knew that she never would have been made a Wolfskin, no matter how hard Rafael had pushed for it.

As she watched the Players wrestle each other around the fire and chatted with Zoe about everything and nothing, for the first time, Jo hardly gave a thought to her stutter.

After dinner, Jo took the path back to the medical center. She had not expected to see Ezra sitting up, his eyes open.

They stared at each other. Then, Ezra smiled loopily and croaked, "My leg hurts," and promptly passed out again.

Jo slept curled up on the floor by his cot until he woke once more before the sun was up. He coughed. He was pale and damp with sweat, but alive.

"Oww. My leg. *Aghh*. That really hurts," he moaned, head back and eyes squinted tight. "I can't look. How bad is it? Will I walk again? You know what, don't answer that, I don't want to be sad right now."

"Hello," said Jo.

Ezra pushed himself up onto his elbows with arm-trembling effort and grabbed his glasses off the bedside crate.

"How long was I out for?"

"About a day."

He made a disbelieving noise in his throat.

"And yet I still feel like someone took a piss on my soul. Cool."

Jo forced Ezra to drink water until her canteen was empty.

"Thanks," he muttered, wiping his mouth.

"I really don't know how you managed to drag me all the way here." He flopped back onto the cot, risking a glance at his stitched-up thigh, and groaned with dread.

"Ez?" Jo said. "Why'd you come after m-me?"

"After you?" Ezra said distractedly. "You mean back in Redgrass?" She nodded.

"Well, they took you," he said, as if it were that simple.

"You s-shouldn't have," Jo said, looking pointedly at his leg.

"What? The gunshot? Don't worry about that," Ezra said. "I was always tripping over both feet anyway. One less to worry about, now. Ha."

Jo pressed her lips into a hard line. People didn't just sneak into a place like Redgrass on purpose. Ezra's smile faded.

"Think of it as a 'thank you' for helping with the radio tower, okay?" he said, then paused.

"Jo," he went on, finally serious. "I actually…found something when I was in there."

The medic stepped back into the room with a tray, and Ezra shut his mouth mid-sentence. He stared at the ceiling until she finished checking his bandage and left again, the door clicking shut behind her.

Ezra leaned back in.

"Redgrass has maps of the whole valley, and all the cities. Everything points to Burning Well." He checked the door again.

"They're waiting until after harvest," he continued. "Then they push. Looks like they already got Kettering. Then they'll go after Roslyn, Suncrest."

He swallowed.

"And Ambridge."

The room tilted. Jo braced her hands on the cot.

Sienna, then. And the General behind her, letting her run ahead and soften the ground. With Rafael gone, there was nothing to slow her down. No one to say no. Kettering was probably already ash.

Ezra shifted, wincing.

"There was more…about Rafael."

Jo froze.

"Seems like Redgrass spotted him, or had him at one point," Ezra continued. "They marked him alive."

The word rang in her head. *Alive.* She didn't let herself breathe too hard. Hope was a bad habit, after all, and one she'd nearly broken.

Still, something warm slipped in through the crack.

"If he's alive," Jo said carefully, "he'd still have the radio."

Ezra frowned.

"Radio?"

She nodded. Ruth's radio. The one she'd carried until the end. The radio Rafael had taken, swearing he'd keep it away from the General. Jo gave Ezra the short version.

Ezra listened, eyes intent behind his cracked specs.

"If that thing's still functional," he said slowly, "and if he's carrying it…then yeah. We need to finish the tower."

"We g-get it working," she said. "We put word out. If he's listening—"

Ezra grinned.

"Then he'll hear you."

20: FIRST CONTACT

RADIO TRANSCRIPT
Location: Suncrest
Receiving: Ambridge

[Static, then a click]

PROPHET: —okay, okay, I'm here. I'm here. Suncrest calling Ambridge. Prophet to Th—oopsies–Gilmore. You there, Gilmore? Cooooome in, buddy-boy.

[A crackle, then—]

GILMORE: Holy hell, you're coming in like hot garbage.

PROPHET: Hey, I'd like to see you put up a tower in one, singular week after getting your leg blown off in Evil Town, USA.

GILMORE: What?! You got your leg blown off?!

PROPHET: Well, not off. It's still there, just not useful anymore.

GILMORE: You're alive, though?

PROPHET: As you can hear.

GILMORE: And sounds like you got the tower up, as poor as the sound quality is.

PROPHET: Sure did! With Crow's help. Like the codename? She did most of the work, actually, what with my leg. But we're alive, the sun is shining, and I can hear you loud and clear.

GILMORE: Huh. Wonders never cease.

[A faint scratching sound]

GILMORE: What's that noise? You got rats in your shack?

PROPHET: That's her. She's drawing some stuff for the show coming up.

GILMORE: Ugh. Owl won't let me out of watch duty, so I can't come see the show. Is it any good?

PROPHET: They're…well, they're enthusiastic. Starling's directing this time, and I think she's really feeling the pressure with so many out-of-towners traveling in just for the performance. We can see 'em camped out outside the wall.

GILMORE: Crazy.

PROPHET: Starling and the rest of the troupe have the Chief helping them out now, so maybe that'll clean up their cues.

GILMORE: She must be pretty desperate to get ol' Chief helping. I would've loved to see those guys yuck it up onstage.

[Scratching noises]

PROPHET: How's the drawing going, Crow? …A microphone right on stage, huh? Looks good. Makes me wish we could record the performance and send it your way, brother. Well…actually…

GILMORE: What are you muttering there, brother?
PROPHET: Can we somehow broadcast the performance?

GILMORE: That would be cool, in theory.

PROPHET: The way you're saying that makes it sound like you think it's not cool. You think Crow's idea is not cool. Go ahead. Say it. Break her heart.

GILMORE: I didn't say it wasn't cool. I meant to say that it's improbable. Your janky mic won't be able to pick up the voices clearly. Factor in the Suncrest audience, who is incapable of shutting up. You'd have to have all the cast in the booth with you, and that breaks all kinds of fire codes, I'm sure…

PROPHET: Yeah, okay, geez. Party pooper.

[A pause]

PROPHET: Man. Can you imagine, though? That would be sick.

21: FOOLERY

Jo liked the feel of pencil on paper. Her notebook filled fast with drawings of the Suncrest amphitheater, the spindly radio tower, the birds in the trees, and even a few crude portraits.

The medic strongly suggested that Ezra stay off his leg, and so the heavier work was left to Jo. Ezra seemed all too pleased with himself as he sat nearby and offered direction, his leg propped on a crate, a blade of grass tucked between his teeth. Jo found it fair, then, to occasionally toss a clump of dirt or a stray pebble his way as she hauled benches into place and helped clear the amphitheater floor.

As they worked, Jo took in every look he threw her way, every smile that felt like the sun. And when he reached past her to grab a tool, she let her skin catch fire and didn't pull away.

Jo found herself looking forward to meals with Ezra and the theatre troupe. They shared bits of roasted apple and joked about their worst flubs on stage. On nights when Jo brought along her notebook and charcoal, they played games of hangman and Drop Me A Line, a cruel exercise the Players had invented to test line memorization. Jo turned out to be good at it, having nearly memorized *Twelfth Night* by then. In a matter of days, her notebook filled with quotes, half-finished games, ugly doodles, and notes passed quietly between her and Ezra.

Twelfth Night crept closer, and the gloom that had settled over Suncrest since the threat of Wolfskins lifted in anticipation. The amphitheater was trimmed of overgrown grass and ringed with logs and benches for seating. Burlap curtains were strung between trees, lanterns hung in the branches until the glen glowed, and instruments were dusted off. The kitchens even broke open an old keg that had been around since before the apocalypse, saved for the night of the performance.

Jo and Ezra took breaks in the shade of the amphitheater while rehearsals unfolded around them. Jo offered to help with signage since her handwriting was steady, mixing paint while she listened to the bustle of voices and movement.

"Places, kiddos!" Norman clapped his hands sharply. "From the top. No scripts."

As the Players scattered, Zoe lingered behind, fiddling with her top hat.

"Thanks for helping us out, Norm," she said.

"A thank you? From Zoe? I'm honored."

"Shut up," she muttered. "I just thought I could do it. But we barely had time to practice this year. There's been so much going on outside, and I know you're gonna think it's silly or not good enough compared to real theatre—"

Norman laughed, a sound Jo had never heard from him before.

"Of course it's going to be silly," he said. "And I hope so. Shakespeare wrote for the people. Sometimes actors got their lines the same day as the performance. To experience any kind of entertainment now is nothing short of a miracle."

He swept his gaze around the glen.

"You've done something extraordinary with your little troupe."

"So you don't think we'll botch it?" Zoe asked.

"You might," Norman said. "But I don't suppose he would've cared."

A drum sounded once from the edge of the glen. The low murmur of the gathering crowd swelled and then hushed.

Norman clapped his hands again, sharper this time.

"Places," he said quietly.

The lanterns dimmed, and the curtains opened.

22: THE SUNCREST PLAYERS

[A tapping sound]

[The audience hushes]

[A violin sails in]

[A hand-written sign appears. In yellow it reads, "THE DUKE'S PALACE"]

[Enter a melancholy Orsino wearing a wide-brimmed hat bedecked with bird feathers and a long cape made of old towels, and other Lords with Curio, with Musicians playing]

[The audience applauds.]

ORSINO: If music be the food of love, play on. Give me excess of it, that, surfeiting,
The appetite may sicken and so die.

[He slumps pathetically onto the nest of pillows, face down.]

ORSINO (muffled): Enough; no more.
'Tis not so sweet now as it was before.

CURIO: Will you go hunt, my lord?

ORSINO (muffled): What, Curio?

[Curio leans in to shout into the nest of pillows]

CURIO: The! Hart!

[Orsino pops up. There is a loud 'thwack' as his head collides with Curio. The audience gasps, then laughs]

A VOICE FROM THE AUDIENCE: Is he okay?

A VOICE FROM THE AUDIENCE: Walk it off!

ORSINO: Why, so I do, the noblest that I have! O, when mine eyes did see Olivia first, Methought she purged the air of pestilence.
That instant was I turned into a hart,
And my desires, like fell and cruel hounds E'er since pursue me.

CURIO: Oh, no. Am I bleeding?

[Enter Valentine, quickly. Curio sneaks off, hand clamped over his nose]

ORSINO: How now, what news from her?

VALENTINE: The element itself, till seven years' heat, Shall not behold her face at ample view,
But like a cloistress she will veilèd walk—

[Valentine pulls Orsino's cape up over his head to demonstrate said veilèd walk. Orsino stumbles]

VALENTINE (cont.): And lasting in her sad remembrance.
ORSINO: O, she that hath a heart of that fine frame—

A VOICE FROM THE AUDIENCE: Her fine frame, eh?

ORSINO: She but hath the finest frame in all of Suncrest!

[Wolf whistles and applause from the audience]

23: DANCE

The air was sweet with honeysuckle as the town gathered in the square to celebrate the spectacular, messy run. The small quartet took their places by the bonfire and wrapped the square in music. The cracked cobblestone in the center of town was transformed into a dance floor, and lanterns hung above like stars on strings.

The banjo struck up, the drummer tapping a steady rhythm on her overturned pail. Conversation about the play rose and fell around them, laughter threading through the music.

Jo dangled her legs off the bench and watched dancers stomp by, the band's guitar strings twanging like bells. Smoke danced and curled up towards a glimmering, clear sky.

When the Players arrived, they were welcomed with applause. It reminded Jo of the old-world celebrities pictured in magazines and how the crowds parted for their arrival. The boy who played Malvolio, even signed a few autographs in his wacky yellow stockings.

"I don't know half these people," Andrés said with delight. "Did you see the audience? Do you know how many out-of-towners we had tonight? Probably fifty at least!"

Zoe was still wearing her moldy costume gown and looked positively radiant.

"What'd you think of the scene change in act two, huh? It actually turned out better than we'd practiced."

"Norm didn't even seem mad that we made up so many lines," Andrés said. "At least the audience seemed to like it."

"You guys killed it," Ezra said.

The band picked up the pace, and the actors started to dance. Zoe pulled Jo into the fray and reached for Ezra, but he held up his hands helplessly.

"Uh, can't. Sorry," he said, not looking sorry. "Super injured over here."

"Loser," Zoe said. "C'mon, Jo. It's easy."

Jo had never, not once in her life, danced. She would have felt more awkward, but somehow, hopping around with people who had been tripping over each other on stage made it easier to join in.

They stomped about the floor, sweaty hands clasped together. Zoe spun Jo around so she felt night air sail in between the spaces where her baby hairs tickled her neck. She hadn't realized her dark hair had grown so much in the past weeks. She also didn't realize she was smiling until the song crashed to a joyful conclusion, and she found her face flushed and her cheeks sore.

Andrés approached the two with cracked mugs of water in his hands. The girls drank greedily.

"Slow song's coming up soon," Andrés said, turning to Zoe. "Save it for me?"

"You don't have to act," she said, smiling.

"M'not," he said. "Might be our last night on earth."

"You say that every time."

Andrés sauntered away to talk to another group clustered by the stage.

"He's such a drama queen. But I do like him, I think," Zoe whispered to Jo. "I see Ezra looking at you a lot. I don't know if you've noticed."

Jo looked away, feeling rather flushed. She'd learned how to disappear in a room, but Ezra made that impossible.

Zoe sipped from her cracked mug.

"It's one of those things, isn't it? It's easier not to let yourself like someone back in case…well, you never know what's gonna happen." Her grin faded slightly. "You ever feel tired?"

Jo couldn't remember not feeling tired. Zoe's steady hand landed on her shoulder.

"But you guys building our tower for us, that's a good thing that's happened," Zoe said. "And then the play going so well…right now I feel like I could punch twelve biters in the mouth. I think it's called hope. Or something."

Zoe's smile returned.

"I'm gonna go dance."

She departed and almost immediately, Ezra appeared at Jo's side to replace her. He jerked his curly head in the direction of the dance floor.

"You, uh, wanna dance?" he said. "Only if you want. And if you, uh, let me lean on you a bit."

Even though he had previously complained about his leg, he limped with her through the other couples, his fingers burning her palm.

The fiddle dipped into a balmy register, the guitar slowed, and Ezra's arm came around to rest high on Jo's waist. His other hand gripped hers, and they did a sort of sway to the slow beat of the song. Jo kept her grip on him tight, both to keep him upright and to keep herself there, too.

"How bout that set, right? Pure magic," he said, gaze drifting past her shoulder. "Norm really pulled it together. And the lanterns—you nailed those. The signs, too. Whole thing wouldn't've worked without you."

They were close, so close that Jo could feel every one of Ezra's soft exhales on the slant of her forehead.

They danced while trying to avoid eye contact. Jo caught sight of Zoe and Andrés dancing a few feet away, their mouths moving rapidly as they conversed back and forth.

Jo licked her lips. How could she express the storm of emotions rolling around inside of her? How could she tell Ezra that she was grateful to him for making her feel seen, even cared about? He cared about what she had to say, and she hardly had to say a word.

"And, uh, I know this might not be the best time, but when is the best time for these kinds of things, anyway?" Ezra was babbling. "Jo, I wanted to ask, if you—"

Through the windows between faces Jo saw a flash of pale hair and a pair of eyes, so familiar and jarring above the circle of music and light.

Jo yanked Ezra by the shirt to block herself from view.

"Whoa—!" he squeaked in surprise. "The leg, *the leg!*" Had she been seen?

"—geez, I literally never know when to zip it, do I? I shouldn't have even brought it up," Ezra was babbling. "You can kick me in the leg if you want. I'll have deserved it if I—"

He yelped again as Jo pulled him off the dance floor, careful to keep herself between him and the place where Nell had vanished.

"But you don't know if she saw you," Ezra said in what was supposed to be a reassuring tone.

Jo paced the floor, stealing one more glance out the palm-sized window. She had tugged Ezra into the small shed and filled him in quickly and quietly. She used the window to keep an eye out for any other Wolfskins prowling around the celebration.

Seeing Nell was like seeing a ghost. Though the months had changed her, Jo had known it was Nell from first sight. Besides her pale face and deep eye sockets that hinted at malnourishment, she looked almost the same except for one thing: Nell's once-long hair that she had prized was chopped as short as her ears. Jo remembered Nell always going on about her hair, how Sienna insisted that if Nell ever became a Wolfskin, she would cut it off.

Ezra grabbed one of the capes hanging beside the costumes and twisted it between his hands.

"You think they followed us from Roslyn?"

"I think," Jo said slowly, "they're d-doing research."

"Research?" Ezra echoed with a nervous look. "Like they want to see what other communities are doing? Like those guys who were spying on Roslyn?"

"Research," Ezra repeated again. "Yeah...I remember them stopping by Ambridge, right before they took Ruth."

Jo's eyes followed the little black spider until it disappeared under the floorboards.

"Hey," Ezra said quietly. "I guess I never asked about Burning Well. I knew Ruth was there, at least for a little bit. But you were there a while, huh? You don't have to tell me. I just—if you want to."

Jo told him. All of it. She didn't stop until the words ran out.

When the story was done, Ezra exhaled, like he'd been holding his breath the whole time..

"I'm so sorry," he said.

She gave a stiff nod.

A thin strand of firelight fell across his golden skin.

"Well, I'm glad you're safe in here," he said somewhat awkwardly, "and not out there with...what's-her-name."

The two didn't emerge from the shed until the moon rose high, and the fires were snuffed out to signal the end of the dance. Ezra slapped one of the costume capes over Jo to hide her, in case Nell or other Wolfskins were slinking around.

They found Zoe and Andrés back at the amphitheater folding up the patched stage curtain.

"We were wondering where you two slunk off to," Zoe said with a cheeky little wink.

But her expression dropped as Ezra explained the situation and asked if either of them had seen someone of Nell's description or anyone else they didn't recognize in the crowd.

"I talked to a blonde girl, yeah," Zoe said, a look of betrayal crossing her features. "She asked if we did traveling shows. I said no, maybe someday. I don't remember her saying where she was from, but Jo, if that's one of your Wolfskins..."

"Did she have sort of bulging eyes?" asked Andrés. "She watched the whole show. I thought she was really into it, so I tried to thank her for coming afterward, but I think I scared her off."

He let out a whistle through his teeth.

"Burning Well, huh? We did open up the show to the general public."

"Burning Well *is not* the general public!" Zoe fumed. "If they're still here..."

But even after quietly spreading the news to the gatekeepers and elders, there was no sign of Nell or any other Burning Well soldier left in Suncrest.

Nell hadn't stayed to fight. She'd stayed to watch.

During their search, Ezra kept looking anxiously at the radio station, the spire stark black through smoke. Jo knew that he was itching to call the others at Ambridge to make sure they were okay. Without a word, Jo took his hand and helped him limp up the hill.

The station was modest inside, no larger than the shed they'd just been hiding in. Ezra sank into the chair, leaned his cane against the close-quartered wall, and went to work on the transmitter. His fingers fumbled with the worn dials as Jo pressed herself against the wall, eyes fixed on the buzzing box.

Ezra called Ambridge again and again. Static answered every time.

"Theo should be on the comms by now," he muttered, his good knee bouncing under the table. "It's his watch tonight."

He tried calling Roslyn, and that worked. Ezra let one of the librarians know that more Wolfskins were spotted in Suncrest. They thanked him for the warning. Ezra hung up and tried Ambridge once again. Nothing but the static spit back.

"I don't understand," he uttered after a good half-hour. "Theo's supposed to be there. He's on the schedule. He's never missed it."

"Faulty wire?" Jo suggested.

Ezra shook his head. "You know Burning Well best, so you can be brutally honest with me, I can take it. Do you think something happened over there?" he asked.

Jo closed the space between them.

"Let's go," she said.

Ezra looked up at her, defeat shining on his features.

"Go where?"

She held out her hand. "Back."

It would take days to walk to Ambridge, and a truck would attract too much attention. Suncrest offered Jo and Ezra a horse. They were packed within the hour and said quick goodbyes to their hosts, to the players, to Norm.

"Come back, okay?" said Zoe, squeezing the breath out of Jo's lungs. "You can be in the next show. I know you don't wanna act, but we're always looking for stagehands. You just have to promise to come back."

Jo hugged her back.

"Promise," she said.

They rode hard without stopping, Ezra holding onto Jo for dear life as she steered their mount on the winding path. They both knew the risk of riding outside the cities with Wolfskins crawling around, but it didn't matter. They stopped when it was light and let the horse drink in gulps from the river, then they set off again.

The closer they got to Ambridge, the more biters crossed their path. Stragglers peppered the woods on all sides, looking so much like trees that it was hard to pinpoint when they were close. It was Spring, after all, and they were everywhere. Jo rode fast and used the bat she kept in her pack to whack at any that ventured too close.

As the foliage grew thick around them and the landscape grew familiar, Ezra tried to reach the Ambridge comms tower with his walkie, but the only sound they were met with was static. Ezra said it was probably just the connection. It wasn't reliable. But Jo could hear the doubt in his voice and spurred the mare onward.

At last, they reached the stone arch, but something was terribly off. Smoke billowed up from the distance, black and rancid. Jo's eyes watered as she slowed the horse to a trot and circled the walls of Ambridge. She wove around arrows which stuck out of the ground like strange plant shoots.

There had been a skirmish, and whether it was the biters or Burning Well, Jo was afraid to guess.

When they reached the front gates, Judee ran out to meet them. Her gaunt face was tight and set. Ezra dismounted first, grunting in pain as he landed on his bad leg.

"What happened?" Ezra demanded, limping without his cane. "Judee, what happened? Was it Wolfskins?"

"No," said Judee when she reached them. "Biters. A whole swarm, like a mass migration or something. I've never seen anything like it."

Judee took the horse's reins and dragged the two toward the gates.

"I'm glad to see you both alive," she said. "Any news of your dad, Jo?"

Jo shook her head and helped Ezra cross the torn-up ground. She pictured tree-tall biters dragging their roots through the Ambridge dirt.

"I'm sorry," Judee said gruffly. "Here, get inside. There are stragglers out here."

"We passed a bunch on our way over," said Ezra, ducking through the gate. "How'd the walls hold up? We tried calling but the line was dead. The biters probably knocked something over, I'm guessing. Theo was supposed to be manning the comms, lazy ass, so I'm going to have to put some kind of fail-safe in place for when something like this happens—"

Ezra stopped and stared at Judee's shaking shoulders.

"Judee? What's…?"

Judee wiped her face with both scarred arms, turned to face him.

"Theo's *gone*, Ezra."

He looked puzzled at first, and Judee had to repeat several times before the muscles in his face twitched with understanding.

"…he was outside the gates when the wave came," Judee was saying, but her voice was distant. "He said something about…about checking a radio line."

Ezra's mouth slackened.

"He wouldn't let me open the gates to let him back inside," Judee continued through a veil of tears. "Not with his bite. He knew he couldn't…It was quick, Ezra. He wanted to make sure no one touched him, or that he…he didn't come back as one."

Judee grabbed Ezra by the shoulders.

"Hey, look at me. I know it's hard, believe me. I'm telling you what happened because it helps to know. Okay? It helps to know."

Ezra crashed to his knees, swearing again as pain shot up his leg. He threw his cane into the gate bars so they clanged.

Judee went to appease the gate guard while Ezra pounded a fist into the dirt. He choked on sobs. His glasses had fallen on the ground but it was too dark to see where they had landed.

"My fault…my fault…" he was stammering. Tear tracks streaked the grime on his face. "I t-told him to check the outside tower. I made him sit there and wait and wait and *wait* without anyone there to watch his back."

He pressed his palms flat against his eyes.

"Fucking idiot. I killed him. Jo, I killed my brother."

"No," said Jo, and dropped to her knees to pull him into an embrace. "You didn't."

Ezra sobbed against her neck and didn't let go. Jo stayed there with him until the ground hardened with cold.

Eventually, dawn came.

Ezra was called to speak with Birdie about funeral plans, so Jo left them to walk on her own. She walked past the arch, not sure where her feet were taking her, not caring. She walked just to feel the earth pound under her soles and remind her that her heart still beat.

She reached the river. The waves lapped softly at her feet.

There was movement in the trees. Then, as though peeling itself out of the thicket, a four-limbed shape emerged, eye pits blooming with bouquets of white flowers, limbs combing through the grass,

Not a biter, not really.

She used to fear the General more than the dodder plant, more than people, more than being bitten.

Living in his house had groomed the fear into her.

But standing at the river and watching the thing in the trees, she knew that fear had changed.

The unseeing bloomer stood in the reflected light of the water's surface. It shed pearly petals as it moved along the flowerbeds.

Theo's death had dragged the fear up where she couldn't push it down again. Losing someone was bad enough. Seeing them come back like that was worse.

Jo grit her teeth. She let her tears fall. She opened her mouth and the sound came out broken and loud.

Her knees hit the soft flower beds. Her head bowed, she waited for it to come and get her.

It never did. It stood like it was made of stone as Jo cried until she could hardly move. Eventually, and as quietly as a deer stepping, it slipped back into the dark of the trees.

The summer had burst hot and humid in the valley. Even the mornings quickly turned from cool to burning in the blink of an hour.

A funeral was held by the stone arch. Ezra stood shoulder-to-shoulder with Jo as Birdie spoke the names of the dead. He didn't flinch when she reached "Theo."

He expected to feel something as Birdie etched the four letters of his brother's name onto a stone, but he didn't. All he felt was the cavern of his empty chest and Jo's shoulder pressing against his.

Birdie set the stones at the base of the arch with the other palm-sized gravestones and the funeral was over. Ambridge felt much smaller as the procession walked back to town.

"I think I'm going to head to the station," Ezra said, leaning on his cane. "His stuff is in there."

He hadn't stepped inside the station since they'd gotten back to Ambridge.

"I mean, to be honest, I don't really want to go in there. Like, ever. But I hate the idea of all his stuff sitting and collecting dust. It's stupid, really."

"Not stupid," Jo said, her eyes flicking to him. The Ambridge radio tower stood tall and wiry against the gray clouds. The handmade *Comms Center* flag sat still on its pole.

"Yeah, it is," Ezra spat, wiping the sweat from under his curly bangs. "You don't have to come in. I might…I might be a mess. Ha, like I'm not already a mess."

Jo didn't give any indication that she thought him messy. In fact, she took his hand. It had a heartbeat, which he felt pulsing lightly on his palm.

"Come if you want," he said brusquely, dropping her hand to open the door, immediately feeling the loss of its warmth. The cold crept back in.

Theo was everywhere. His stack of *Gilmore Girls* VHS tapes sat by the wall, still missing season six. Candy wrappers lay crushed underfoot, ash clinging to the plastic. Ezra used to joke that Theo was more likely to die from old food than a biter attack.

The place was dark and suffocating, full of junk stacked to the ceilings. Useless junk. His hand itched, so he grabbed the closest object—a headset he'd spent ages fixing up—and threw it against the wall. It gave a satisfying *crack*.

"My stupid, scheming, never-shut-up brain!" Ezra growled, snatching a box of Theo's candies and hurling them against the wall, too. Nerds spilled and pittered on the floorboards. "I just had to go off and build my damn towers. I had to have a platform. For *me.*"

Throat sore from screaming and hands hot from clenching them, Ezra slumped into the desk chair, his cane clattering to the floor. He wouldn't cry, not again. He didn't want to think about how Jo was looking at him.

"It should have been me here," he whispered, lips trembling. "It should've been me."

"Ezra."

He could barely lift his head, but when he did, Jo was standing at the desk. She didn't look afraid of him or nervous of another outburst.

The radio on the far shelf crackled once, then fell silent again.

Her face was full of determination as she moved her hand towards the player, extracted the tape inside, and handed it to him.

Ezra stood up on his good leg, breathing hard, and tilted his head to read the blue scribble of Theo's pen on the strip:

LOG 136

ideas by theo.

(gilmore girls and what coffee tastes like)

"I didn't make this," Ezra said dumbly.

Jo turned back to the cassette player, popped the tape inside, and shut the little plastic door.

"You…you hit the *Play* button," Ezra instructed numbly.

She did.

Click.

And then, they waited.

26: IDEAS BY THEO

RADIO LOG 136
Location: Ambridge

[A click]

THEO: Testing 1-2-3? Okay? Yeah? I think it's coming in pretty clear. I wanted to spitball and didn't feel like writing, so here I am.

Also, I made the executive decision to name our radio show. If that bothered you, Ez, then you should've been here instead of gallivanting off to do the exciting part of building the towers. Someone had to stay and run the comms here, and that sacrificial someone was me, okay? So you can't complain that I'm taking up tape space or whatever. You can always record over it.

Title. A title. I know we were talking about a few, and they were okay, but we can think bigger. Think Stars Hollow big. Think *Gilmore Girls* big.

I have an ongoing list of all the places and important thingies that go down in the show. At first, I was thinking about Luke's Diner, how it kind of serves as the space between places, like a place where people come and go and stay to rest or get one of those cups of coffee Lorelai never shuts up about.

They always made coffee look so good on the show. Every time I watch it, I just crave that weird brown juice. Those Gilmores guzzle it down like it's water. I've never had it myself, but some of the older folks here get this dreamy look in their eyes when they talk about it.

Birdie said it wasn't even that good, actually, but it was the rush you got whenever you drank some. I don't care if it tastes like dirt, I'm getting some, somehow, someway.

[A scribbling sound]

Just making a note to call Suncrest again before you leave, Ez. They just might have some.

Okay, next one: Friday Night Dinner.

See, this one isn't a place in the show, but the Friday night dinners were this obligation that Lorelei had to go to every Friday in order to appease her mother, right? She doesn't want to go every week, but she does anyway. But then it ends up kind of rekindling their fractured relationship.

I don't know what that's got to do with our broadcast, but that's an idea, too. Like I said, I'm spitballing.

I guess I should be grateful that you at least watched the first season with me, so we have something to talk about.

You remember how our running joke was that people in the show didn't put liquids in their cups? They're always gesturing with these empty ass cups, which supposedly have coffee in them, but we know. We have eyes. So, what, did people in the old-world just carry around empty cups for fun?

Do you remember when Samson was alive, how he used to carry a container to spit his tobacco in? Freaking nasty, but dude, what if that's what the Gilmore girls were doing? Did they need something to spit their fake coffee in?

Anyway, while you're off doing that tower stuff, I had to get to the bottom of it. Birdie is way too full of knowledge about the show, so we hang out after dinner and she tells me all about how these old shows were filmed.

She told me that T.V. people would record the same scene over and over and over again, like hours and hours of the same part. Which is crazy because I always just assumed it was like one of the Suncrest shows, where it's one and done. Sometimes, it took them days to film one thing. Days.

So, if they put real coffee in the cups, the Gilmore girls would be bouncing off the walls and would need to pee every other second.

Days of filming one scene. Man. They must have had a lot of time back then.

I forgot to tell you to keep a lookout for season six while you're out there. I know Norman doesn't have *Gilmore Girls* at the library because I called him as soon as the tower was up. Maybe our twin telepathy will get this message to you. Or I can just call again once *Twelfth Night* is over.

Makes me wish I could go see it. I keep telling Suncrest that they need to take their shows around to other towns. Maybe they'll come here next.

In the meantime, just tell me about it once you and Jo are back. And I know I was being an ass about it, but it would be cool to get something like that playing on the radio. Don't know if that's possible. Probably not. But we didn't think this was possible, either. Who knows?

With all the trouble we're going to, we've got to make the show happen, right? I don't want you coming back to Ambridge all, "Unh, my ideas are stupid and I suck," like you always do. It's not all about you, you know. Maybe I want to yack in people's ears and say things that make them laugh. Maybe I just want to talk about a show I like. Birdie may be my only fellow fan, but I'll bet there are a bunch more middle-aged ladies who appreciate it as much as I do. We just gotta reach 'em.

It's been quiet here without your constant yapping, actually. Too quiet. Yeah, take the compliment. Whatever. Shut up.
So, a title.

Apocalypse Train.

[A pause]

A-POCK-a-lypse Train.

[A pause]

Yeah, I'm still thinking on it. It has a ring. I might like it. So jot that down, brother.

[A click]

27: SHOWTIME, AS THEY ONCE SAID

Ezra was still staring at the player when they reached the end of the recording. The shack filled with the muffled sound of gears still turning. Jo hit the *Stop* button. Theo's voice settled over the musty room.

"Huh," said Ezra, for once at a loss for words. Jo was looking at him with her big, dark eyes.

The tears came fast and messy. Ezra dragged his sleeve across his face and shook his head once, like he was trying to clear water from his ears.

"Your dad," Ezra said suddenly. "The broadcast. I promised I'd put the word out." Jo nodded.

"Then maybe we should do it," he went on, more brazenly. "For Theo, for your pop. I mean, we might as well try, right?"

Jo didn't mention that Birdie wouldn't like it, and didn't mention that the hope of finding Rafael now had dissipated.

As Jo had predicted, Birdie looked at Ezra like he'd asked her to do a backflip.

"And what does that mean, exactly?" she said.

"Since Project Tri-County is complete," said Ezra, "and we're able to contact all three communities now. I wanted permission to do a live show."

Birdie leaned on her cane and frowned. She'd injured her knee during the wave.

"A live show," she repeated, limping across her office to sink into her desk chair. "Well, if something like that was possible, what would it be?"

Jo nodded encouragingly for Ezra to go on.

"News, music, messages between our communities," he said. "Live." Birdie studied him.

"We can try it once," he added quickly. "If it's a mistake, we stop. And it wouldn't cost us anything except some power, which we have. And we have it in abundance since Jo here fixed the windmills."

"Ezra," Birdie said.

"We've already done the work, Birds. Theo and I talked about it all the time."

Birdie's severe shoulders seemed to loosen at the mention of Theo's name.

"This thing safe?"

Ezra blinked.

"Is it…?"

"I don't want news about us available to whoever listens in," she said.

Ezra dove into his knapsack, swaying on his leg so that Jo nudged him to keep him upright.

"We use codes," he was saying. "Only for certain details, like names and places and events and times. Think about radio used during the Old World Wars—your time, of course—or when the military used to keep us updated in the first few years. Only our towns have the cheat-sheet."

Birdie took the proffered water-stained notebook and flipped idly through it.

"Nothing too complicated code-wise," Ezra said. "We'll be safe, and we can run everything by you before we ever broadcast."

"Ezra."

"This was all Theo's idea first. He made some sort of comment back before we even fixed up the Ambridge station. All he wanted was something to listen to while he worked, something that wasn't me talking, ha-ha. He tried rigging up the little television and cassette player in the station so he could watch *Gilmore Girls* while he tinkered on things, but you shut that down pretty quickly when you saw we swiped it from the events center—"

"*Ezra,*" Birdie repeated firmly.

At last, Ezra pressed his lips together to shut himself up. Birdie handed back the book.

"Code names for everything."

He nodded.

"Code names for everything."

Birdie tilted her head. "What about Theo's and my show, hmm?"

A small smile glimmered on Ezra's tired face.

"There's a *Gilmore Girls* segment," he said. "Good," said Birdie. "We can give him that, at the very least."

"Can I trash Burning Well?" Ezra added. "Not by name."

"No, Ezra."

"They're clowns, Birdie."

"I'm letting you have this," Birdie growled. "Don't push it."

The morning after the Birdie negotiation, Jo made her usual trek up the hill to the radio station and had to pause to take in the sight: a single-file line of people. They were all standing and chatting amiably in the morning light. One of them had a stringed instrument tucked under her arm. What were they all waiting for?

"Ah, thanks," Ezra said hungrily as Jo handed him a baked potato from breakfast. "Jo, could you let in the next batch for me?"

Jo gestured to the line outside the door.

"What's this?" Ezra chewed thickly and answered with a sticky grin, "Auditions! I wanna see if the quartet who played in Suncrest is available—didn't you like them? And I need a co-host."

At that moment, Judee bustled into the station, looking very frazzled. She had little white feathers peppering her muddy jeans and boots.

"Jo, can I grab you?" she barked. "The door on the chicken coop came off, and I need someone to hold it while I screw it back in."

"Jo's helping me," Ezra protested.

Judee rolled her eyes.

"She's just being nice, Ez. Why don't you go make yourself useful and chase a chicken while me and Jo do the heavy lifting? As. Usual."

"Hey, we're doing important work here, too. Entertainment lifts spirits, raises morale, makes us believe in something," Ezra said smoothly, to Judee's irritation. "And it looks like you can catch the chickens yourself."

"He's terrified of chickens," Judee told Jo with an evil smile. "So how about you get off your butt, Ezra, and I won't lock you in the coop. How's that?"

"What a-about her?" Jo asked.

"What about me what?" Judee said.

Ezra squinted through his foggy glasses and stood up slowly. "Huh," he mused.

When Jo came back from the coop, Judee stood by the microphone with her arms crossed while Ezra explained the controls.

"I must be out of my mind," Judee said.

There was electricity in the air on the night of the broadcast.

Ezra paced the room, humming up and down the floor. The musical quartet sat shoulder-to-shoulder on the moldy sofa, harmonizing under their breaths and giving their instruments a final tune. Even Judee looked anxious. She sat in the back corner, hands balled into fists.

Ezra spun around in his chair to face her.

"All done?" he asked anxiously.

Jo had spent the evening handing out radio receivers to the guards on the wall and making sure the speakers in the community center were working properly. She'd tuned them all into the frequency Ezra had given her.

"Great." Ezra beamed. "I've radioed ahead to make sure both Roslyn and Suncrest are tuned in. Anyone with a receiver could hear it," he added. "All seems to be working, all systems are go."

Jo cleared the rasp in her throat, feeling very tall and awkward as she looked down at him in the chair. It took him a moment to slow down his fiddling of the radio knobs and face her. She'd grown comfortable with Ezra, more so than anyone, probably. But the question still sat on her tongue and refused to budge. She took a steadying breath.

"I know it's a long shot," she began, "b-but I wondered if we could…could…"

Ezra's gaze softened. He stood up, removed a sheet of paper from his small stack, and slipped it into her hands. She scanned the page.

"Already in the lineup," he told her. "I put a message in there for Rafael. I don't think I can say his name on the air, so if you could just look it over and make sure it sounds right, or add in anything specific you'd like me to say. But I promised I'd put the word out for your dad way back when we were building the towers. That felt like forever ago, huh?"

Ezra stood up, a head taller than her.

"This is the very bare-minimum, absolute least I could do for you. Is it okay? Or should I—"

He stopped mid-sentence as Jo threw her arms around his neck and gave him a hug she hoped communicated all the gratitude and affection she felt bubbling up for him in that moment. She released him quickly. Ezra blinked, startled, then smiled.

"U-uh, well! Look alive, people!" he said, clapping his hands as Jo took her spot on the comms to observe the connection. "We go on air in five minutes!"

"You owe me," Judee said. "Big time."

"You'll get your cigarettes," Ezra said silkily, sliding on one headphone. "After you do the show with me."

There were minutes on the clock until action. Ezra spun in his chair to address the ragtag crew taking up space in his office.

"This is it," he said. "Showtime, as they once said. Let's make it good because it's the first—and possibly last—show Birdie will ever let us do. Let's give off some light."

He flipped the switch.

28: APOCALYPSE TRAIN

RADIO TRANSCRIPTION
"APOCALYPSE TRAIN: Broadcast #1"
Location: Ambridge

[A folksy tune played on banjo eases in]

PROPHET: Gooooooood evening, and thank you for tuning into Apocalypse Train! I'm your host, Prophet, and with me tonight is Saint Jude. Say hi, Saint!

SAINT JUDE: Hello.

[Music fades]

PROPHET: She's really excited to be on tonight, listeners. She's even prepared a little song for us.

SAINT JUDE: Don't push it.

PROPHET: Kidding, kidding. Tonight's broadcast is the first of its kind, and hopefully not, but quite possibly, the last. We've got a great lineup for you all. Our goal is to bring a little news, a little connection, and a little light for these dark nights. How was that for an intro, Saint?

SAINT JUDE: Do you want me to be honest, or do you want me to be nice?
PROPHET: C'mon, it's my first time.
SAINT JUDE: Then it didn't sound cheesy at all.
PROPHET: That's what I like to hear.
SAINT JUDE: And if none of you can hear us right now, well, we'll have the recording we can pass around later or something. Right?

[a pause]

You did remember to press the button, right Ez—I mean, Prophet?

PROPHET: Yes! Wait…Um. [Shuffling sounds] [Unintelligible]

SPEAKER 1: …crap…don't tell me you…
SPEAKER 2: …is the signal even going out?
[Unintelligible]
SPEAKER 3: Oooooh man…
SPEAKER 1: …zra!…counting on…just been sitting here talking to no one like an idiot…I'm going to—

[Unintelligible]

PROPHET: Wait a sec—okay, my uh, producer Crow here says it's all good. Yes! It's fine, it's all fine! I knew I pressed the thingy. We're good.

[Relieved laughter]

PROPHET: Whew! Close one. And a fantastic transition for us to get things rolling with the news.

[A banjo theme plays]

[A sound of rustling paper]

PROPHET: Now, it's no secret the Werewolves have been running loose out there under the light of the full moon. Most of our listeners know firsthand the damage they've caused to our triad.

SAINT JUDE: The Werewolves don't attack first. They drive biters toward the walls and watch who responds first, and who panics. Our source says they take who they need. Fighters first, even children, then women, and then anyone who can work.

PROPHET: If you hear knocking after a wave of biters, don't answer. If someone offers protection in exchange for people, don't bargain.

SAINT JUDE: We are not his slaves, and we will not be taken. And remember that they need you more than you need them. When we stand together, we're strong.

PROPHET: Well said. I'd like to invite you all into a moment of silence for the friends and loved ones we've lost to the recent attacks. Tonight, we honor Toby Evans, Sally Chen, and Theo Singer of Ambridge, who all recently passed away while defending their home city. This broadcast was his idea. We were supposed to do it together. I hope this…this suffices. Love you, Theo.

[A solemn silence]

SAINT JUDE: Thank you. We now have an urgent message for a lost person. For privacy, we will refer to you as "R": your daughter is alive. She asks you to remember Catch-22 and stolen coffee by the handful.

PROPHET: If you're the person our dear friend is looking for, make it known. I'm not really sure how we'll do that without risking our location. Our friend is here in the studio tonight. If she would like to…?

[Rustling]

[A long pause]

A QUIET VOICE: …I'm going to f-find you. P-promise.

PROPHET: Thanks for looking out, everyone. Keep our friend in your thoughts and your prayers. At this time, we'd like to bring a little light and move to our next section I'm calling "Art and Shakespeare in the Time of the Zombie Apocalypse." Too much, Saint?

SAINT JUDE: Much too much.

PROPHET: Would it be me if it wasn't much too much?

SAINT JUDE: Guess not. So my sheet says that this is the part of the show where we talk about community goings-on: art, shows, recent discoveries, and whatever else our friends have been doing to keep themselves sane.

PROPHET: That's right! And what better way to kick us off than with the smashing success of Suncrest Player's recent production of *Twelfth Night!* I was in the audience that night, Saint.

SAINT JUDE: How was it?

PROPHET: I wouldn't be surprised if this version of *What You Will*—which is the other name for the play, don't ask me why, that's a question for William himself—won every theatre award that exists, it blew all the other plays out of the water.

SAINT JUDE: All the other ones, huh?

PROPHET: Yes, ma'am. The Suncrest Players really pulled out all the stops. That's something the Werewolves don't bother with. Music or plays or people gathering for no reason except to be together. I always thought it was integral to our survival, alongside eating and sleeping and avoiding insane warlords and parasitic plant monsters.

SAINT JUDE: I heard there was audience participation.

PROPHET: Yes! It was a rip-roarin' good time full of flubs and audience participation and one apple core thrown at Malvolio. We, uh, don't encourage that so much as the verbal participation, but it was an experience all the same.

PROPHET [cont.]: I guess the second project to mention is…well, this broadcast! Exciting, isn't it? It's like we're right there in the room with you all, in all our crackly-voiced glory.

[Rustling]

SAINT JUDE: huh? What's this for?

PROPHET: Just read the paper.
SAINT JUDE: Uh, "Say, it's feeling a little cramped in here. I wonder why that is? I'll leave that explanation to my wonderful co-host—" This is stupid.

PROPHET: Aaaand that's because we've got a special treat for you all tonight! A fantastic acoustic quartet! Wanna say hi, fellas?

[An overlap of greetings from GUITARIST, BANJO PLAYER, and DRUMMER]

PROPHET: I heard you play at the after-party. Fantastic stuff. So glad you could make the trip, what with the outside world being the way it is.

BANJO PLAYER: How often do we get to broadcast our chops?
DRUMMER: Not very.
PROPHET: Well, let me scooch over for you, and I think we're ready to roll. Listeners, please enjoy.

[Movement, shuffling]

[A shaker counts in, followed by the strumming of a guitar. The violin sails in softly]

In the moonlit night, beneath the sky, There's an old black train, rolling by. Through the twisted woods and trees,
It carries secrets on the autumn breeze.

Through valleys of sorrow and hills we climb, Our lantern lights the path of grime.
Beware the shadows that dance and sway,
In the golden fields where the lost ones stray.

Through the valley of friends we knew, Hollow eyes with daisies bloom.
In the late-night hour, let the whistle blow As we ride on tracks where the mem'ries go.
So carry me on, through the shadows and light, Old black train, through the night.
Riding on echoes of the lonesome rail, On the old black train, through the veil.

[Silence]

[Light applause]

PROPHET: Thank you, all of you. We're so glad you came on. Hopefully, this will be the first of many.

VIOLINIST: Thanks, bud. We hope so, too.

PROPHET: Well, folks, that just about does it for us. Thank you for tuning in to Apocalypse Train. I don't know when it will be possible to broadcast again, but if the tracks are clear, we'll be back.

SAINT JUDE: Remember that silence works better for them than it does for you. And if you're listening, you're already connected.

PROPHET: Stay safe out there! Thank you and goodnight!
[Some shuffling]
[The sound cuts]

29: ANSWERED

"Wow! Ah! I can't believe it. I'm shaking. Look at my hands, I'm shaking!" Ezra gushed. "What did you think? Be honest."

Jo allowed herself a heartfelt grin and gave him two thumbs up.

"I've never been that scared, holy shit," said Judee, who had her arms wrapped around her own chest as if trying to hug the breath out of herself. She was grinning, too, and looked so much younger as she grabbed Jo and gave her an excited little shake. "Do you think the signal went through? Could we check with the other communities or…?"

There was a hum of consent, and Ezra tripped over his own feet as he flung himself back to the desk. He unplugged the aux cord of the headphones and turned a few dials.

"Roslyn? You're speaking to Prophet, did you just try to call in? Please tell me you heard the broadcast. Over."

Some silence, then static, and then, *"Roger, Ambridge. We heard you loud and clear. 'Fact, we got everyone crammed into the library here listenin' to it or watchin' me interpret for the ones hard of hearing. You're gettin' a round of applause as I speak."*

Another bout of static, then an unintelligible chorus of voices and what might have been clapping.

"Y'hear that, Prophet? Over."

"Yeah," said Ezra, and he quickly swiped his eyes with the back of his sleeve. "Loud and clear, Roslyn." Before he could sign off, the radio stuttered unintelligibly.

Ezra frowned, and turned a dial.

"Roslyn, were you trying to say something? Over?"

Static…"Roslyn?" Ezra said.

"…Heard, Ambridge," came a clipped voice.

Ezra's hand froze in midair. Then he reached for the dial and turned it completely off.

"Who was that?" Judee asked.

A deep crease formed on Ezra's brow.

"I have no idea," he said.

The applause lingered, then thinned. People drifted back into the night in small clusters, chatting all the way back to town. Ezra limped back to the radio station to take up his post on comms. Jo joined Judee on the wall for the watch, and the two munched on sunflower seeds and basked in the aftermath of the broadcast.

It was after midnight when the land went still. The crickets quieted. An owl stopped mid-hoot. The only sound was the gentle crackling of the torchlight.

"Come in, wall flowers," came Ezra's voice, distant on the walkie. *"Just making sure you're both situated up there. And—uh—weird thing, don't be alarmed. But we picked up another signal after the broadcast. Couldn't place who it was from. Over."*

"Great," Judee replied stiffly. "Not one of ours? Do you think someone intercepted? Over."

"I mean, anyone with a working receiver can tune in, so yeah," Ezra replied. Jo gripped her rifle and stared into the black eyes of the forest.

"But we were careful. Codenames come in handy, and the people have to know," Ezra said, *"And Saint? Thanks for doing that with me. It was...awesome. Over."*

"I know I didn't do Theo justice," Judee replied. "But it was fun. Over."

"No. It was perfect." A pause. *"Is Crow there? Over."*

Judee handed the walkie over. Jo clicked the talk button a few times to make her presence known.

"Hey," said Ezra. *"I really do hope tonight did something and that your person comes around. But if he doesn't—either way, I'm really glad to have met you. Yeah, I know, I think I'm feeling extra sappy now that it's all over. But I really can't imagine not knowing you, so I'm glad for that. Uh, yeah. Confession alert, ha-ha. There you go. Over."*

No matter how hard she tried to form the words, Jo's mouth moved noiselessly. Before she could respond, tell him that she felt the same, and thank him for putting the word out for Rafael, there was a loud and sudden cry from somewhere in the woods.

A high-pitched howl. A warning. A call.

The line on the walkie crackled into silence, and Jo planted herself into a crouch, her blood pumping at full capacity and rushing into every corner of her body. She could see a small company of ten or twelve peering out from the trees, and so nightmarishly familiar that Jo felt her stomach lurch in horror.

"Jo?" Judee asked, her fist raised for the wall to hold fire.

A lean figure separated themselves from the pack, a white kerchief clutched in a gloved hand.

"We don't have to make this harder than it needs to be!" the woman called from below. Jo recognized Sienna's bark anywhere.

"Back again, are we?" Birdie demanded in her low drawl. Jo hadn't seen her appear beside Judee, her chin raised high.

In what was probably supposed to be a show of good faith, Sienna removed her mask and raised her hands up. Her coils of red hair fell out and framed her hard, smiling face.

"We're here on behalf of Hayes," she called. "General of Burning Well."

"Yeah, we know him," spat Judee. "He stole our people already, and now he wants more?"

"We're here to offer terms," Sienna continued.

"So talk," said Birdie. "Or move along."

Sienna lowered her arms slightly.

"Burning Well needs recruits. Hayes is offering warm beds, protection, plenty of food, and the best training you'll get anywhere. We know multiple surrounding communities have been hit with the biter waves in the last few weeks." Her steady gaze drifted over the top of the Ambridge wall as though she didn't have a handful of guns aimed at her head.

"General Hayes's goal," Sienna continued, voice rising in bravado, "is to create a world safe from the biters—the real monsters. His walls are impenetrable against their waves. Not one of our people has been bitten in years. Redgrass has already joined our family. Kettering rejected Hayes's offer, and now their city sits smoking in the earth.

"Ambridge has resources," Sienna went on amongst murmurs. "Your people, your infrastructure, and a broadcast capable of reaching beyond its walls." Her teeth reflected yellow in a sheen as she smiled at her Wolfskins, along the wall and past the place where Jo crouched. "Come peacefully, and assignments will be made. The General will create a new human race, a race that in future generations, will be immune to this parasite." She paused. "Those selected will be transported tonight."

And then, because she didn't want to hear another word, because she didn't want to hide for one more minute, Jo stood up from her hiding place, small next to Birdie but not feeling so. There was a ripple of shock and outrage from below.

"Raf's girl!" shouted Tom.

Birdie kept focus on Sienna. "We know what your General does at that fortress of yours," she said. Her response seemed to give more courage to the rest of the Ambridge watchmen because they all started to shout things:

"We're not interested in joining his war," said Judee.

"Or his harem!" said another.

"Justice for Ruth!"

"I'd rather be bitten."

"This is your last chance to talk peacefully, Ambridge," Sienna said, her voice drowned out in the insults.

"Then you'd better take your people before the noise draws the biters right to you," Birdie boomed. "Don't come back again."

Sienna's face broke into one of the most terrifying grimaces Jo had ever seen. Then, there was an explosion of noise as the Wolfskins descended on Ambridge.

"Open fire!" Birdie roared and sparks lit up the night in bursts. Jo took aim on the lip of the wall and pulled the trigger, but the Wolfskins were dark and quick as shadows.

Jo snatched the radio off the crate and ducked again under a shower of splintered wood. She spammed the Talk button.

"Ezra? E-Ezra?"

A crackle. A blip. Then, *"…o…w…are…coming…"*

Jo kept the radio clutched in her hand and tried to think through the firefall. There were only a handful of Wolfskins at the gate, but as Jo knew, there was a good chance that the rest were hiding in the cover of the trees. And, Jo remembered, there was also the matter of—

"Tear gas!" someone screamed.

Jo and Judee ducked through a chorus of coughs.

Through squinted eyes, Jo could see the Wolfskins' gas masks gleaming like fish scales. Teen recruits, no doubt. She wondered if Nell was down there, too. There was a cacophonous noise as a bit of the wall blew up. Concrete showered overhead.

"Stand your ground! Don't let them through!" Judee's face was blackened with soot, one eye swollen shut as she fought through the dust cloud. "There! At the gate!"

Jo turned in time to see Big Tom, gas mask pushed up into his greasy hair, an unlit explosive clamped between his ugly teeth. He'd tried to blow up the wall, and now he was going straight for the door. Jo wiped her nose, took aim for the head, and *pop.*

He slumped onto the ground, dead.

"Nice shot!" Judee said.

There was a brief moment of elation as the two looked at each other. Then, Judee's smile froze in place as something crashed into the back of Jo's head.

Her vision burst with spots. A protest floated in from somewhere on the edge of her consciousness, but it felt miles away. Jo felt her body leaving the ground, suspended in the air. Her shoulder crashed against metal ground as she was thrown into the back of a Burning Well truck.

"Jo!" Judee shouted.

Another body was thrown in beside her, heavier. The door slammed shut.

"Tie the woman first," came a voice, muffled by the hum of the engine.

Judee swore. There was a scuffle and fabric tearing. When Jo's eyes adjusted to the dark, she could make out Judee tied on the floor opposite her, something stuffed rough into her mouth.

There was a lurch as the ground fell from under her. The truck was moving. Beside Jo lay Ezra, curled slightly on his side. His face shone with blood.

She looked up toward the cab. A Wolfskin sat at the wheel, his weak jaw circling as he chewed.

"That's the radio boy," he said. "And Raf's girl. Tie 'em. Orders are alive."

Jo and Ezra found each other in the dark. Ezra gave a small nod, his glasses flashing once in the moonlight.

The man in the passenger seat turned around, a curved metal bar in his hand.

"Hold still, kiddies," he said. "We don't want to break you."

With that as his cue, Ezra sprang forward and launched himself at the man. They wrestled for the crowbar. Jo leaped to help. She managed to reach the driver's seat and plunge her fingers into Tom's eyes. He screamed.

The steering wheel spun and the truck lurched. Jo's stomach dropped. An explosive sound like metal on metal broke through the dark as the door to the driver's seat flung open. Gravity yanked her into the night.

"Jo!"

She crashed into the icy depths of the river, and for a moment in the muted underwater of the riverbed, there was peace.

Jo broke the surface, coughing and spluttering, the tide yanking her back down as she watched the truck grow smaller and smaller on the bridge above.

Then it was gone.

III: SUCH DISGUISE

VIOLA
Conceal me what I am, and be my aid For such disguise as haply shall become The
form of my intent. I'll serve this duke.
Thou shalt present me as an eunuch to him. It may be worth thy pains, for I can sing
And speak to him in many sorts of music That will allow me very worth his service.
What else may hap, to time I will commit.
Only shape thou thy silence to my wit.

CAPTAIN
Be you his eunuch, and your mute I'll be.
When my tongue blabs, then let mine eyes not see

—Shakespeare, *Twelfth Night*

30: GARMENTS

Jo thought she must be dead.

She had landed on a river bed up to her elbows in mud. Something stung like a cut, but she couldn't tell where. She felt so thoroughly exhausted that she thought of resting her eyes and succumbing to sleep.

It was the sound of moaning that jolted her awake and the groan of biters approaching that made her scramble to her feet. In stomach-dropping horror, she saw that she had fallen right into a deep glade lush with moving foliage and lumbering biters, yellow curling and twisting around them like tangles of yarn. Eyeless sockets peered out at her from the darkness. A human shape with broken limbs and covered in flowers gave a shuddering rattle.

She had fallen deep into the valley, where the biters had been left alone.

Jo had no weapon and nowhere to go. She crouched by the riverbed as the infested area closed in.

She felt the familiar shot of panic course through her veins as one of the biters turned and made its way toward her. She fumbled in the mud for a rock or a stick—anything to defend herself with—and reared back as the rotting, bluish human face looked down at her.

What happened next was so opposite to what Jo was expecting that she thought she'd bumped her head. The biter, who was draped in a layer of moss, peeled itself back to reveal…

…a person. A living, human person.

He was young, no more than twelve years old, and skinny, and he was wearing a cloak of reeds and moss peppered with flowers, with a disembodied biter head perched on the top to create a very convincing illusion.

There was a rapid movement of biters catching the whiff of her scent. Jo shuffled backward, so her boot splashed in the lip of the river.

The boy lifted a long finger in front of his lips for quiet. Then, he raised the hem of his strange garment and ushered Jo under it.

Against her better judgment, though there wasn't much room for it now, Jo stooped underneath the mossy cape and was surprised to see that there were hidden folds that created room enough for both her and the sinewy boy to fit comfortably. Jo followed his lead, and together, imitating some sort of shambling half-dead thing, they shuffled right into the nest.

It was the most bizarre thing Jo had ever experienced, like moving in a dream. She could peer through the fibers of the cape and look right up the broken nostrils of a biter as if she was invisibly moving among them.

The flower-headed bloomers were docile and didn't give them a second's attention as the two shambled past as slowly as a real infected would.

They left the clearing without a single biter following them, but they kept the disguise in place until they reached a small, packed path. Then, the cloak was removed.

"Your name?" the boy asked, attention fixed unswervingly on Jo's face as if she was a creature he'd never seen before. He had round cheeks and bare feet. He couldn't have been more than thirteen years old.

"Jo," she breathed.

He just stared at her. Then, he began walking. Jo followed. They walked for a good portion of an hour in silence, slow enough that Jo could keep up with her swollen ankle. The dawn had just broken and cast the wet forest in a purple haze. The shadows of trees stretched like long fingers across their path, and soon, they came upon a small village. It was unlike the cities and walled communities above the valley. Tiny tent-like shelters were crafted around clefts in the rocks, under canopies, or leaning against proud tree trunks. Fire smoke tinged the air, and Jo could see many of those strange biter garments hanging by the doorways of every domicile.

Jo's companion ventured ahead a few feet and disappeared inside the flap of one of the tents. Jo stood swaying on the spot, not knowing whether she was supposed to follow or to stay put.

Then, a man emerged, carrying a rifle. He had always had graying hair, but his beard had grown long and full with flecks of silver running through it. He took one look at her and dropped the gun.

"Jo," said Rafael.

He ran forward, and embraced her.

"My baby girl," Rafael said. He cried over her head. Jo found herself crying, too, her back shaking with sobs.

The boy set the two up inside the tent and left them to talk alone. Jo and Rafael sat close around the hearth. Rafael told his tale first. It wasn't long, and Jo suspected he left out a lot of details about his hardship.

He told her about how, after being shot, a wave of biters came down into the clearing and scattered the Wolfskins before they could finish the job. He traveled for days, nearly got caught by Redgrass after sneaking in for some food and bandages.

Then the rains came.

The mountain shed water, and the biters came with it, moving downhill in a slow, dragging mass, drawn by the wet ground and the growth breaking through it. Rafael said he'd tried to hide, but the wave carried on around him, rooted limbs pulling past his body.

"I thought that was it," he said. "Figured I'd been left just long enough to die anyway." Then, one of them broke off from the others.

He shook his head, like he still didn't quite believe it.

"It was a person. Under one of those cloaks," he said. "Couldn't believe my eyes when it turned out to be one of the folks here. The boy."

"The cloaks," Jo said, unable to stop herself from interrupting. "H-how do they…?"

Rafael chuckled.

"It's a mystery of nature to me. They said it's something they learned from the bloomers—y'know, the really flowery-lookin' ones? Something about their flowers having a calming effect."

While he talked, Rafael placed a hand on his side, and Jo suspected it was a mortal gunshot wound that brought him down.

"Lots of bloomers down here," he continued. "The folks cut off bits, make the cloaks. The cloaks allow 'em to pass through. Wild place. Absolutely wild."

Jo looked around at the tent. The fabric walls moved gently in the breeze.

"So the folks took me in, patched me up," Rafael said. "I been helping with security and whatever else. They're good people here. Quiet, keep to themselves. Odd, but really smart, I'll give 'em that."

Jo settled deeper on her cushion. There was a small firepit in the center of the room and bedrolls neatly stacked in the corner. It looked practical and earthy, ready to be picked up at the first hint of danger.

"My plan was to go out and find you as soon as I could walk again," Rafael continued, "but there were Wolfskins and Redgrassers lookin' for me, and I was weak. I looked for you, I did. But then I thought you might have been dead already, and I…" Rafael shook his great head, mouth lined with anger.

Jo took his calloused hand in both of hers, afraid that if she let go, he'd vanish. Rafael's gaze kept drifting to the corner of the tent.

"Jo," he said, quieter now. "That radio you picked up, do you remember?

"Yes."

"We turned it on down here," he said. She leaned forward. "Never expected much. No one's signaled in years, so I didn't have hopes. Until last night," he ran a baffled hand through his graying hair, "the signal suddenly got stronger. Last night, loud and clear, we heard music. And then, I couldn't believe it—I heard *you.*"

Jo blinked a few times, unsure if she'd heard correctly.

"You…you heard the…?"

"No one here could believe it. We were getting music again, and news about what was going on upside." Rafael said with a sort of awed laugh. "And I knew it was you the second you spoke. Thought I was dreamin'." He had tears in his eyes and didn't bother wiping them away.

He wanted to hear Jo's story, so with her voice quiet but steady, she told it. She told him about finding Ambridge, the library, Ezra, Judee, the radio towers, the play at Suncrest, and the broadcast. At last, she described the siege.

Rafael listened without interrupting. When she finished, he drew in a breath and held it.

"I should've told you sooner," he said. "Burning Well has radios."

Jo looked up.

"They don't use them," Rafael went on. "Haven't in years. But they kept trying. Tried to get someone to fix the systems, even tried to get a tower up before. But they always put it off."

He grunted, careful of his side.

"Hayes didn't think it was urgent," he said. "Not until now. He heard the music, your show."

Jo stared at the packed dirt between her boots. She saw Ezra at the mic, the light on the board switch on.

"They took him because he can m-make it work," she said.

Rafael swore under his breath.

"You've been through it," he said after a moment. "I heard they were seizing communities. Taking young people. Women. That's Sienna's way."

"She came h-herself," Jo said.

Rafael let out a short, humorless breath. It pulled a wince from him.

"Figures." He stared into the fire. "She came down here, too. Not long before you did."

Jo looked up in alarm.

"I couldn't fight," Rafael said. "I could barely stand." He stared into the fire. "They took people, though. I should've done something. But I didn't want Sienna knowing I was alive…"

Jo hesitated.

"How d-did the boy outside know me?"

"I told them I'd lost my girl," Rafael said. "Asked them to watch for you. Said you might not talk much. But you sure seem different."

He gestured to her dark, natural hair, which she'd let grow a little. It framed her face in small curls. "You're all kinds of different, Jo," he said in quiet wonder.

She straightened under his proud eyes. She wasn't sure when the change had happened exactly. But like the cloud cover breaking to let the sun poke through, she could feel it.

Rafael forced Jo to rest her ankle for a couple of days while they talked through a course of action. But Jo was antsy. Ezra and Judee were being carted into Burning Well while she sat in the valley.

And Ambridge…she needed to know what had become of Ambridge. But she couldn't break into Burning Well, even with Rafael's help. The place she had grown up in was a fortress. Her brain hurt with impossible odds.

While she feverishly tried to think around obstacles and come up with a semblance of a plan, the boy who brought her, who introduced himself as Fox, offered a good distraction and took Jo to the gardens.

She had never seen so many flowers in one place before. Burning Well kept the surrounding trees burnt and trimmed so as not to attract biters. The valley was the opposite.

Then, the shadows between the trunks peeled out and walked forward.

"Bloomer," Fox said and ushered Jo towards it.

She stared at the bloom of the old biter's head. There were no eyes or a mouth to bite with. They'd been replaced with a bouquet of orange butterfly weed and long cardinal flower stalks. The creature swayed there and let the butterflies, honey bees, and hummingbirds flutter around its limbs.

"They help the crops grow," said Fox, pointing to the roots in what was once the bloomer's feet. "And keep biters nice."

Jo asked Fox if he'd seen biters with arms like tree roots, like the one she and Ezra encountered in Roslyn.

Fox gave a low whistle. "Roots," he said. "Nasty. Deep roots. They can grow anywhere."

Fox then showed her how they fashioned their garments from cloth, then added bloomer cuttings to spread their roots through the fibers. The result was a lush cloak of tangled flowers and foliage. At the end of each wear, he explained, they set the cloaks flat on the ground and watered them to keep them thriving. It was tricky work, the cloaks, but with Fox's help, Jo was able to put together one of her own.

"Are you going to the bad place?" Fox asked as he helped her weave in the bloomer flowers and toss a handful of seeds into the damp fabric.

Jo nodded. "They t-took my friends."

Fox's eyes were like dark, unblinking pools.

"Mine, too," he said. "And my mom."

"Sorry," Jo said.

The boy continued to help her water the leafy cloak until a thought popped into Jo's mind.

"C-can we make more of these?" she asked him.

He looked thoughtful about it. Then pleased.

"Enough to walk where they won't."

Rain came in the night, hard enough to swell the river and turn the paths to mud. By morning, the valley swelled with water. Streams rushed downhill, and so did the biters.

A whole horde of them moved down the mountain in a loose stream. They followed the wet ground, with their feet dragging and heads bowed. The flowers on them hung heavy with water. Everyone knew biters grew fat when it rained.

Jo stood at the edge of the village with the others and watched the horde pass, scraping trails of mud as they shambled downhill.

Fox stepped close and handed Jo the cloak.

After taking a steadying breath, she pulled it on. It lay heavy on her shoulders, cool and soft with moisture. The flowers brushed against her jaw and a drop of water trailed down her neck.

"Slow," Fox prompted. "Like them."

They stepped onto the path together. The biters whispered around them.

One passed close enough that Jo could see the split bark of its arm and the pale shoots pushing through skin. She held her breath beneath her mossy hood.

Without glancing at her, it continued downhill with the rest.

Jo matched its pace. She let her weight sag and dragged her feet through the mud, just like Fox had taught her.

Her heart hammered in her ears. She waited for a hand to close on her, or teeth, but nothing happened. She and Fox walked through the stream and stepped out on the riverbed, out of the glen.. Only then did Jo let herself breathe.

"They follow the water," Fox said, pointing. "Where things grow."

Jo watched the last of the biters disappear into the trees. The path behind them lay open and quiet.

On the day of the trip to Ambridge, Jo and Rafael rose early and ate slowly, warming their hands on too-hot cups of water and staring blearily into the fire. She watched as the village slowly rose, packed bags of food, and secured weapons on their belts. Rafael stuck the radio into his bag and loaded his handgun. Fox was giving the bloomer cloaks they had made a last sprinkle of water. Jo hoped the garments would survive the trip.

"We don't go looking for trouble," one of the folks said, taking one. "But we don't leave ours behind."

She watched their faces reflect pale orange from the sunrise and was stilled by the memory of the last time she'd seen Rafael all those months ago and the girl she had been then.

She cringed at the memory of her first days at Ambridge, how she was so scared of being without her protector that she'd shut her mouth completely. She cringed at the memory of when she used Ezra as a biter distraction. He never would have done the same to her, even if the stakes were high enough to demand it.

Jo felt the tickle of a warm breeze on her cheeks. Ambridge was like that. And so was Roslyn, and Suncrest. The people looked out for each other in ways that made no logical sense to survival.

She pulled the cloak tight around her shoulders.

She wouldn't hide again.

Ambridge was silent upon their arrival. The party of four walked along the broken pathway over deep tire tracks left by Burning Well's trucks in the mud. Upon seeing the cracked gate, Jo rushed ahead of the party to bang on the bars.

The gate opened slowly. A boy stood on the other side, eyes red, and rifle too big for his hands. "Birdie's dead," he said.

Jo's lips parted in disbelief. She'd never expected the indestructible Birdie to fall. Jo looked around at the faces around her and felt her heart sink.

"Who's that?" the boy asked, jutting his rifle into Rafael's chest.

"Rafael," he introduced brusquely. "Mind letting us in? We've got a long road ahead, and we could use all the help we can get."

They were ushered to the town hall, and upon entering, they saw that the cabin was completely full. Jo stepped in to see half of the Ambridge folk whispering on benches or huddled by the hearth.

"Jo!"

Jo barely had time to take in the room before Zoe was on her. She'd leapt up from the long, wooden table and rushed the door. The rest of the Suncrest Players followed with embraces and murmurs of relief. She received a nod from Norman and a rush of greetings from Ambridge folk.

"Someone radioed as soon as the Wolfskins took you all away," Zoe said, breathless. "We came straight over. You have no idea how crazy things have been since the broadcast."

Across the room, Rafael and Norman shook hands and began to speak in careful voices. Zoe leaned in.

"They came to Suncrest," she said. "The day after you and Ezra left." She lowered her voice so Jo had to lean in.

"Sienna and a few Wolfskins," Zoe went on. "They didn't take anyone, but they did ask a lot of questions. About us." Her thin mouth tightened. "About the theatre."

Jo blinked, surprised.

"They said someone had *recommended* us." Zoe exhaled through her nose. "Nell, obviously. She stayed after the show, talked about how good it was and how people should see more of it."

Jo reached for the bench behind her and sat without realizing she'd moved. The room felt suddenly louder. Nell's face floated up in her mind.

Zoe fingered the scraggly ends of her hair.

"We played dumb and said we just perform where we're told. They camped nearby for a day. Didn't threaten us or anything, just hung around." Zoe watched Jo's face for a reaction. "Then Sienna said the General might like a performance, and she'd be in touch."

"And?"

"And they left," Zoe said. "And then the broadcast happened. We didn't want to be waiting when they came back."

Jo's gaze slid to the door. The shadows beyond it stretched long and dark across the threshold.

It was then that Rafael stepped forward, straight-backed and severe. The room quieted without him asking.

"We're going to Burning Well," he announced. There was a ripple through the hall.

"It's not smart, but they took our people, and we intend to get them back." He locked eyes with every corner of the room. "If you come, know there might not be a return trip."

"I don't want to burst your bubble," Norman interrupted, white eyebrows furrowed. "But the walls are impenetrable, aren't they?"

"I'm open to suggestions," Rafael said, turning to the crowd of young Ambridge, Roslyn, and Suncrest folk. "Jo and I have lived there since the beginning, so we know there's one way in and one way out."

He was right. Even when she was living there comfortably up in Hayes' house with the brides, Jo remembered exploring the rigid grounds, winding her way down every passage and alley. There was a protective bunker he kept to himself, which of course all the brides knew about. But as for any sort of secret exit, Jo knew of none.

The hall muttered, spitting ideas at each other. Jo wished Burning Well had a sewer line like Redgrass did, just to give them a fighting chance. Ezra had traversed that sewer line to save her. She had to return the favor, somehow.

"We rush the gates like they did to us," said Andrés. "We climb the walls." "Dig under the gate."

"We could take a hostage," Norman suggested coldly. "If we catch them off guard, that'll help," Rafael said.

"A distraction?" offered Norman. "They bragged so much about never seeing any biters at their door, but what if we brought the party to them?"

Rafael suddenly turned.

"Fox."

The boy looked up, cloak hanging from his thin shoulders.

"What about the biters?" Rafael asked.

Fox thought for a moment.

"They move when the water moves."

The talks went late, so Rafael built fires in the fireplaces and distributed apples and nuts for roasting. Even Fox joined the throng and showed them how he liked to crisp up the apple skins and eat them like chips.

"Zoe," Jo said in an undertone.

Zoe wrapped her hands more snugly around her dandelion tea.

"Have you all ever t-traveled?" Jo asked. "Have you performed in other p-places?"

Zoe blinked her round eyes.

"No," she said. "We've always just done our plays at Suncrest."

Jo thought of Nell in the audience that night of the show, *watching*. The memory brought back a wave of fury. A Wolfskin inside the crowd, learning the rhythm of the place, where people entered, how the guards moved, or what doors stayed unlocked after dark.

"Does Burning Well have theatre?" Zoe asked. "Or books?"

Jo lowered the tip of her stick into the fire, and the flames licked it black.

"Only the G-General," Jo said. "He keeps the b-books to himself. No one else is allowed t-to own them."

Zoe turned the apple in her hands, worrying at the skin.

"Maybe Nell just wanted to see one," she said. "A play, I mean."

The apple slipped from her fingers and hit the floor with a dull thud.

Jo pictured Burning Well's bare buildings and people sitting with nothing to do but wait. She thought of Nell slipping away from the Wolfskins, just to sit quietly in an audience and watch a story unfold.

"Burning Well is s-starved," Jo said. "For anything like that." Zoe didn't answer right away. She stared into her mug.

"I don't know what we'll do if we don't go," she said finally. "If we don't perform, they'll just come back and take us. But if it's a trap to get us into Burning Well…" She aimed a hard kick at the apple. It went spiraling and disappeared under a table. "We're screwed either way."

"Catch-22," Jo said.

By the time the fires burned down, Jo had a seed of an idea forming in her mind.

She wouldn't call it a plan, yet. It was reckless and probably fatal, but it was something that wouldn't let go, even in her dreams, long after the hall went dark.

31: SHAPE THY SILENCE

It was a hasty two days of preparation, packing, planning, and leaving very little time for doubt to creep in. Jo didn't lay her idea out cleanly, but she didn't have to. Rafael clocked her, read her like a book, and filled in the rest.

Fox and Rafael handled the outside work. Sound carried differently in the valley, and especially after a rainfall. The timing mattered, and so did sound: buzzers to push biter hordes in a direction, cloaks to tag along without being bitten. Jo listened when they talked about signals, and the windows where things might line up.

Might was the keyword.

Fox's people laid cloaks out on the ground, damp and green, more than Jo had expected. Fox pulled one over his head and ushered both Jo and Zoe underneath. They all fit when they pressed close.

There weren't enough cloaks to save a whole city, but enough to move a few small groups at a time.

Inside the hall, Norman worked the Players hard. He ran scenes without costumes, then with them. He made them enter and exit until the movement felt casual and unremarkable. He told them to slow down when they rushed, to keep their eyes up. He told them they belonged, and their performance would be just like any other.

Zoe adjusted blocking to account for guards. Andrés practiced lifting props with one hand, keeping the other free. Stagehands learned how to break the set down fast and quiet, how to move it without drawing attention. They practiced reaching into the costume racks and pulling the mossy garments free, ducking under them two or three at a time. They rehearsed until they were vanishing in front of Jo's eyes.

When they couldn't justify waiting a moment longer, the Suncrest Players loaded their props, costumes, and set pieces onto a wagon and followed Rafael out of Ambridge. They passed beneath the stone archway and onto the forest path, leaving the fires behind, and began the long walk back toward Burning Well.

They made camp before dusk. The ground was soft from recent rain, the air damp and fresh.

Somewhere downslope, biters moaned as they moved with the runoff.

When a small horde drifted close to the path, Fox pulled one of the cloaks over his shoulders. A dried biter head sat loose at the crown. He stepped off the path and into the horde.

The Players gasped. Zoe even tried to go after him, but Jo tugged her back, holding up a hand. *Wait.*

The biters enveloped Fox into their line, bumping once against him before adjusting. Fox moved with the current, the dried-head swaying limply to mimic the others around him. Jo even lost sight of him at one point in his camouflage.

Then he bobbed back to the group, as though a bush had decided to come over and say hello. Andrés exhaled the breath he'd been holding.

Before they broke camp, Fox and the valley folk handed every third Player a folded garment. They were damp and heavy, alive with seed and stem. They packed them carefully alongside their costumes.

"Walk slow," Fox instructed. "Like them. Stay together."

When, at last, they came to a forest of burned trunks and floors of black pine needles, the company stopped, and Rafael announced that it was time to disperse.

"Jo?" he said, turning to her. She stood to attention. "Got your walkie?"

She brandished one of Ezra's radios she'd grabbed from the shed, his name scribbled on the back in slanted, yellow ink.

He checked his handheld buzzer, though they'd already charged the batteries before leaving Ambridge.

"You'll be okay, right?"

Jo slipped Ezra's radio back onto her belt and paused. She closed the space between them and hugged Rafael around the middle. She inhaled the scent of his green jacket: canvas, earth, a musty scent, and she burned it into her memory.

He hugged her back, and kissed the top of her head. "Give 'em hell."

Raf, Fox, and the other valley folk broke off while the Suncrest players huddled and watched them disappear under moss garments, heads bowing into the mist until they vanished completely.

The cliffside was quiet. The wind shook the pines.

"Well," said Norman quietly, as though afraid he might disturb something. He turned to Zoe. "Any words for us, madame director?"

"Jo?" Zoe asked, voice a little shaky but her stance steady as she faced the Players. "How far are we?" Jo could remember how these same needles crunched under her boot. "Up the h-hill," she replied. Zoe nodded with some difficulty. "Then you should get into costume," she said. "And the rest of you, just think of this as another audience. Captain Rafael will be doing the hard part, getting the biters to move this way, and we just have to do our thing, then get out. Got it?"

"If we don't die a horrible death, first," mumbled Andrés.

The once-rowdy party quieted with nerves and readied themselves to cross into Burning Well territory. Jo, who knew she would be recognized in the city, stepped aside and let them work.

They dressed her in loose men's trousers and a shirt. Someone smeared grease paint along her jaw and dotted her chin with rough stubble. Zoe crushed a hat down over her curls and tugged it low.

"Your disguise," Zoe said.

Jo took the mirror when it was offered. The glass was cracked down one side, and she barely recognized the person looking back. Her dark skin was dirt-streaked. The scar along her face paled at the edges, but her face sat differently now. There was nothing soft left for anyone to grab.

She adjusted the hat and weight settled into her stance. Shoulders sloped. Head dipped.

"That'll do," said Zoe.

"Our princess is in disguise," Norman declared, addressing the party. "And remember, no improvising tonight, if you can help yourselves."

With everything in place, Jo steeled herself and led the company up the hill and into the house of the General.

The guards at the gate did not look surprised to see them approach.

One of them scanned the brightly painted wagon. His eyes lingered on the faces of the Players–Jo was tucked safely behind Andres.

"You weren't told to come today," he said.

Norman inclined his head.

"We come when we're called," he said evenly. "Actors don't choose the hour. We always show up ready."

The guard studied him a moment longer, then turned and shouted up the wall. The doors screeched open.

Trying not to look either euphoric and terrified, the Suncrest Players, their cart, their bag of tricks, and their hidden princess stepped through the gates.

The city hadn't changed. They were escorted at a measured pace along the central road. Concrete buildings rose on either side, pale and bare. Young soldiers were everywhere, all matching in their grey camouflage. Some were barely older than Jo. Their boots struck the ground in time, a steady rhythm she remembered in her bones.

But they stopped to watch them pass. Their eyes were fixed almost hungrily on the wagon, on the flashes of fabric and wood and color.

From the far end of the square came the sound of scuffling, and a crack of something striking flesh. Jo didn't turn her head, but she knew the training arena by sound alone. She had scrubbed blood from that floor.

The concrete tower rose ahead of them, its shadow cutting across the street.

Jo's gaze followed it, just long enough to take in the narrow windows, and the place where the brides were kept. She thought of Snow. She thought of Faith, her hands braced on her belly. She would have given birth by now. Would the General keep her, even when she couldn't give birth anymore?

Jaw clenched, Jo adjusted her hat and kept her stride even as they passed beneath the tower and into the square. Whatever this night demanded of her, she would meet it.

They were met in the square by an officer Jo recognized.

"The General looks forward to the performance," he said. "He's asked that you consider staying on, if the night goes well."

Norman thanked him politely, without committing to anything.

Guards remained as the Players unloaded the wagon and hung the curtains. Norman's voice drifted through the space as he assigned positions and spoke to passersby, calm and mild, as if this were any other town.

Burning Well had never hosted an event, and by midafternoon, word had spread.

Jo counted the guards as they worked. She marked exits and entrances, recalled paths and planned a route of her own.

Somewhere deeper in the city, Ezra was still alive.

They wouldn't kill him, they needed him. Rafael had told her the General kept half-built projects alive out of spite alone, kept men breathing just to see what else he could wring out of them. Ezra would be working, or being made to work. Jo kept that thought close.

Judee was harder to place.

Judee was a fighter, and would not go quiet. Jo pictured her angular shoulders, her mouth full of teeth, her defiance, just like Ruth's. The thought that the General might have dragged her upstairs, might have decided she belonged with the brides, made Jo's jaw lock.

The stage stood at the center of the square, boards already laid and the curtains tied back. There were far too many guards. As dusk fell, the square filled. There were no families or children, no one but the

General's finest in attendance. Wolfskins clustered near the front and soldiers packed in behind them. Others stood along the edges, their boots planted wide, waiting for a show.

Torches flared to life one by one. Light climbed the concrete walls and washed over the balconies.

Beyond the city, past the watchtowers, the treeline sat dark and unmoving. She fixed her gaze there and waited for the signal Rafael had promised.

Movement rippled through the square, and a space opened where there had been none. The guards suddenly straightened, and the crowd shifted with unease. Jo kept her eyes down and counted boots when a door opened above the square.

She didn't need to look up to know who it was.

The General stepped onto the balcony of the council building. He rested his hands on the stone rail and looked out over the crowd, slow and deliberate, as if taking inventory. The noise died down almost instantly.

When his gaze finally dropped to the stage, it slid past the Players and moved on.

Hidden beneath the brim of her cap, Jo kept her gaze fixed past the walls. Somewhere out there, Rafael would be watching the same sky she was. Somewhere under this city, Ezra was still alive.

Zoe gathered the Players behind the curtain.

"No one breaks character," she said quietly. "No matter what."

Jo drew a breath, pulled her cloak close, and waited for the cue.

32: TWELFTH NIGHT

"TWELFTH NIGHT"
By WILLIAM SHAKESPEARE with THE SUNCREST PLAYERS
Transcript

[A tapping sound]
[The audience hushes]
[A violin sails in]

[A hand-written sign appears. In yellow, it reads, "THE DUKE'S PALACE"]

[Enter a melancholy Orsino wearing a ridiculous hat bedecked with bird feathers and a long cape made of old towels, and other Lords with Curio, with Musicians playing.]

ORSINO: If music be the food of love, play on. Give me excess of it, that, surfeiting,
The appetite may sicken and so die. Enough; no more.
'Tis not so sweet now as it was before.
CURIO: Will you go hunt, my lord?
ORSINO: What, Curio? CURIO: The hart.
ORSINO: Why, so I do, the noblest that I have! O, when mine eyes did see Olivia first, Methought she purged the air of pestilence.
That instant was I turned into a hart,
And my desires, like fell and cruel hounds E'er since pursue me.
[Enter Valentine]
ORSINO: How now, what news from her?

VALENTINE: The element itself, till seven years' heat, Shall not behold her face at ample view,
But like a cloistress she will veilèd walk And lasting in her sad remembrance.

33: CONCEAL

The audience was nothing like Suncrest.

They didn't laugh much, but their silence was so complete that even the birds didn't interrupt.

Wolfskins filled the front row. Jo stayed just inside the shadow of the curtains and watched them instead of the crowd. Tom stood near the front with his same scowl. Their attention stayed fixed on the stage, on the actors' voices carrying into the square. No one spared a glance toward the wings.

That was what she needed.

She slipped away from the stage and kept to the darker paths between buildings, choosing dirt over stone where she could. She reached for the walkie at her hip and lowered the volume, turning the dial with careful fingers. Rafael's signal would be loud when it came.

She was easing it down when a voice stopped her cold.

"…extremely disrespectful, Sienna. I'm sure you know that."

Jo screeched to a halt, heart slamming into her ribcage. She ducked behind a stack of medical supply crates, praying she hadn't been seen. But she knew the voice, she knew that silhouette.

General Hayes stood in profile, a dark pillar against the stone. His hair had gone gray at the temples, his coat pressed and clean. His eyes glimmered like black rocks in a riverbed.

"I didn't mean to pull you away from the performance," Sienna was saying. "You asked me to report."

"And?"

"The Players arrived earlier than expected," she said. "They came without notice." Hayes's mouth curved, faint and pleased.

"Artists are like that," he said. "Always eager to be seen."

Sienna hesitated. "Do you want them housed after the show? Or sent back out?"

"I want them kept," he said. "Comfortably, at first."

Sienna nodded. "Of course."

"They'll agree to stay," Hayes went on. His gaze drifted back to the crowd in the square. "If they don't, we'll make arrangements."

"Yes, General."

"There's no need to rush," he added. "Let them finish the play. I won't interrupt art." A swell of applause rose from the square. Hayes watched it with quiet satisfaction. "After," he said. "We deal with them after."

He took a step towards the square, then stopped.

"And check on our radio tower," he added. "I want that system live tonight, if possible."

"I sent Nell," Sienna said.

The General's angular mouth quirked, and Sienna stiffened.

"I suggest you make sure she's where you told her to be," he said. "If you can't keep track of your apprentice, that reflects on you."

Sienna stood for a few tense seconds after he left.

"Get out here. Now," she said.

Jo's blood ran frigid. There was nowhere to run without being spotted, and even so, if Sienna had known where she was hiding all along, why hadn't she alerted the General?

But just before Jo could make any move at all, another figure stepped out of the shadows. *Nell.*

She stopped short when she saw Sienna, hands half-raised like she'd been caught mid-theft.

"Sorry," Nell said. "I didn't mean—I was just—"

"Zip it," Sienna hissed. "What are you doing here? I told you to stay with the boy."

"I did," Nell said quickly. "I checked on him. He's still down there, and still being difficult." She swallowed. "I just wanted to see the wagon."

Sienna looked ready to strangle her.

"Why?"

"Well, there was nothing in it," Nell said, words tumbling over each other. "Except costumes and stuff." "Why were you *snooping?*"

"I didn't tell you to–" Sienna hissed again.

"Because of Jo!" Nell said in a high voice. "I told you! I *saw* her. In Suncrest. Right after the play, I saw her dancing. I thought she must be here with them, and if she is…"

Sienna laughed, unkindly.

"You're still on this?" she said. "You see ghosts everywhere you look."

"I know what I saw," Nell insisted. "And if she's here, then they're not just here to–"

"That's enough." Sienna stepped in close. "You're not a Wolfskin, Nell. You don't think like one, you never have. And you still can't hold a gun straight."

Nell's mouth fell open, tried to form words, closed again.

"I'm tired of covering for you," Sienna went on. "Go back and make the radio boy get it working. If he breaks something else, I don't care how you handle it, as long as he's breathing and that system comes online."

Nell nodded, brimming with tears.

"Yes, Captain."

"And Nell."

Nell froze.

"If you pull me away from the General again," Sienna drawled, "I won't protect you next time." Then she disappeared the way she'd come.

Nell stayed where she was, breathing unevenly. After a moment, she lashed a kick at the dirt and sprayed pebbles. She slipped down a side street and stumbled into the stretch of the city. Jo trailed her. The stage noise thinned behind them.

Nell stormed past the training arena, swiping tears, muttering, and went through a gate with *Under Construction* marking the chain link. Jo crouched by the fence, willing Nell not to glance in her direction. But Nell looked adamant, her eyes focused on the ground. She wrenched open a door in the ground, and disappeared through it.

Jo waited a full minute. The wind was soft and silky. She was far from the stage, and she couldn't catch wind of the actors' lines anymore.

Jo checked her walkie again. Still no signal yet. She stood back up and went after Nell.

There were voices echoing up from the dark hole, too garbled to make out. Jo hesitated. If she went down, she might very well be trapped.

Then Ezra screamed. The sound hit her like a shove.

Jo grabbed the ladder and slid down, skin burning as her palms scraped the rungs. The space below was cramped and bare. Wires ran along the ceiling and disappeared into the metal door.

"Get the panel working *now.*" Nell's voice cracked sharp through the dark.

Jo stepped into the spill of light from the open hatch and knew she was standing at the base of a tower—a radio tower. She had never known that's what it was for. The shaft was narrow and unfinished, the walls raw concrete, wires tacked in place with metal hooks. She could hear the hum of a generator somewhere.

"If you touch that again, I swear to God, I'll take another finger." Jo could see Nell's back, shaking.

She'd always had trouble with her aim.

"Please," Ezra said. "Please, not again. I'm trying. I am."

He was pressed against a panel of dials, his hands splayed flat. His voice didn't sound like his anymore. It was high, panicked, foreign. His fingers were splayed against the wall, like a butterfly pinned to a board, and Jo could see two very bloody stumps where his right pinkie and ring fingers should have been.

Nell stood a few feet away, a gun braced in both hands.

"You think I like this?" she snapped. "You think I wanted this job? The General wants it live tonight, and you keep breaking things."

"I'm not breaking them," Ezra said quickly. "It's not calibrated. You can't just power it up without—"

"Shut up." Nell took a step closer. "If you don't get that transmitter running, or whatever it is, I'm done making excuses for you."

Ezra swallowed hard. His eyes flicked behind Nell, then dropped to land on Jo.

"Do you understand what'll happen if you shoot that thing in here? Huh?" Ezra was saying. "Those bullets will ricochet off the walls! Right back at you. How's that for karma? Tell you what, you get me out of the hole, and I won't even try and run away. Last time was different. Promise. Just put that thing down, and we can mosey up the–"

Nell gripped her gun in both hands, and Jo inched towards it. Her fingers brushed through the pillar of light.

"Shush!" Nell said, flustered. "Maybe if you'd have shut up, we'd be done and you could've kept your fingers!"

Jo put a finger to her lips where Nell couldn't see, and Ezra gave a minuscule nod.

"—and maybe I'll tighten the cuffs all the way. How 'bout that?"

The pistol left Nell's hands in a clean arc. Nell staggered back, more startled than hurt, and turned just in time to see Jo step fully into the light.

"You—!"

Ezra broke from the wall like a piece of shrapnel. He brought his foot down onto the back of Nell's knee. She crumpled to the ground and Jo was already there, the gun steady against Nell's head.

Nell gasped, hands flying up.

"Do it," she sobbed. "Just do it.

Ezra stared at Jo with cold dread. He looked worse up close. Bruises and cuts lined his face, and one eye was swollen shut. He quivered on his bad leg and his missing fingers were wrapped in dirty cloth, stiff with blood.

"Jo…" he said in wonder. "I didn't even know that was you for a second. What with the hat and the…" he trailed off, his gaze going to a snotty, simpering Nell. "What do we do now?"

Jo knew that there was an obvious answer, though she didn't like it. She could admit to times where she wanted to punch Nell in the mouth. But seeing her all crumpled down there, Jo felt pity.

When Jo spoke, Nell flinched as if she had clicked the trigger.

"Where's Judee?"

"Who?" Nell whined.

Ezra clenched his good fist.

"Judee!" he said. "The woman you took from Ambridge."

"I wasn't *in* Ambridge, dickhead," Nell sniffed. "I didn't even like doing that kind of stuff." Jo pressed the barrel into Nell's forehead.

She screamed.

"Nell's in the medical bay!" she said. "But they keep a watch on her at all times. Don't let her near weapons."

Jo exhaled. That figured.

"Any others?" Ezra pressed. "Who else have you taken?"

Nell hesitated.

"Some from Kettering, and I think few from the smaller places. There's so many, I don't even know…they do orientation first, at the barracks."

Once again, Jo checked her walkie. Rafael should have radioed with the signal by now, so where were they? The Players could only stall for so long—two more acts, last she heard—and Jo still had to get to the tower, to the brides…

"We can't l-let her loose," Jo said decidedly, and Nell's eyes grew wide. "You wanna…?"

Ezra began, nodding to the gun, looking a tad nauseous.

Jo relaxed her hand, barely.

"Nell," she said slowly, "Can you g-get into the General's house?"

Nell hesitated.

"Yeah," she said. "I mean, I have a key, I bring up food sometimes or new brides, if we got 'em."

"Jo," Ezra said cautiously, "what are you planning on doing?"

Jo explained as much as she could, about the plan, the cloaks, the play, Rafael, but knew they were running out of time.

"We need to g-get Judee," she said. "Anyone they t-took. And we have to g-get out before the wave hits."

"Then we need to move them quick," Ezra agreed.

Jo nudged the back of Nell's head.

"Help me get into the t-tower," she said, "and I'll l-let you go."

"Yippee," Nell grumbled. "We'll be extra trapped when the biters get us."

"There's a safety bunker in the t-tower," Jo told her, patience thinning. "For Hayes and his b-brides and children."

"He has a whole *bunker* for himself?" Nell said. "Why didn't you say so? You take up so much time trying to get your damn words out, you didn't mention–"

Nell let out a tiny squeak as Jo gave the gun a warning *click*.

"She's right," Ezra said. "If you go into that tower with the wave coming, you'll be trapped. What if you can't get back out?"

"I'll be okay," she said, pretending she believed it.

"Jo, I…" he said. "I can't lose someone again. And not you," he went on. "Especially not you."

"We have to m-move now," Jo said stubbornly.

Ezra glanced past her, toward the ladder and the dark mouth of the shaft beyond it.

"No," he said. "You go."

Jo opened her mouth to argue.

"I can't run with this leg," he told her. "And I can't fight like you. But I can do this."

He tapped the side of the control panel like it was an old friend.

"This reaches everywhere."

Nell scoffed.

"You're dead the second you turn that on."

Ezra didn't look at her. He was already crouching at the panel, already pulling a cable loose. His hands shook, but they didn't slow.

"That's fine," he said. "It'll spread the word faster than I can move. People deserve to hear it."

Jo stepped towards him. "Ez—"

"They deserve a chance," he said simply. He turned back to the panel and flipped a switch, then another. The lights along the board flickered. "Get Judee, prisoners, the brides, whoever you can. As soon as you hear me, double-time it."

"We gotta go," Nell hissed, bug-eyes grazing the horizon.

Jo dug in her bag and thrust her garment into Ezra's hands.

"Put it on when you hear b-biters," she said. "And when Raf gives the signal."

Ezra frowned.

"Signal?"

Jo unclipped the handheld radio from her belt and pressed it into his palm. His name was still scratched on the back. She closed his fingers around it before he could argue.

"He'll t-tell you when the biters are moving," she said. "Wait for that. Then you talk." Understanding settled in Ezra's face.

Before she stepped back, he reached out his long arms and embraced her. He felt thin but warm. Jo's heart did a little flop as he pressed his forehead flat against hers.

"Be safe. Please?" he said.

Then, he kissed her. His lips were gentle, like wings fluttering briefly against hers. Fire spread from her face to her toes, and she was pretty sure she kissed him back.

After he broke away, Ezra threw himself to work. With a wrench in one hand, he cracked open a panel and sent wires spilling at his feet. A speaker grill buzzed with feedback. The radio crackled softly in his grip as Jo left him with the cloak, and the promise of a signal.

34: TWELFTH NIGHT (AN INTERRUPTION)

"TWELFTH NIGHT"
By WILLIAM SHAKESPEARE with THE SUNCREST PLAYERS
Transcript

[Viola, dressed as Cesario, crosses the stage. Feste follows, tapping a tabor]
VIOLA: I saw thee late at the Count Orsino's.
FOOL: Foolery, sir, does walk about the orb like the sun. It shines everywhere.

[Scattered popping sounds carry over the wall]
SOMEONE IN THE AUDIENCE: Do you hear that?
SOMEONE ELSE: That's not right.

VIOLA: Nay, an thou pass upon me, I'll no more with thee. Hold, there's expenses for thee.

[She gives him a coin]

FOOL: Now Jove, in his next commodity of hair, send thee a beard!

[Another sound; long and groaning like an ocean. A siren starts, then stutters, and stops.]

SOMEONE IN THE AUDIENCE: What is that?

SOMEONE ELSE: Look at the wall!

FOOL, quietly, as he exits: I will conster to them whence you come.
[Backstage, a whisper]
FOOL: Jo's not back.

SOMEONE ELSE: Ezra isn't either.
FOOL: Then keep going.

VIOLA: This fellow is wise enough to play the Fool—

[A siren cuts]

AN AMPLIFIED VOICE: People of Burning Well. Please remain calm.
A minor disturbance is being handled.

[Gunfire cracks from up on the walls]

[A strange buzzer sounds from over the walls]

AN AMPLIFIED VOICE: There is no cause for alarm. Please remain in
your–
A VOICE IN THE CROWD: There! A horde of them! At the gates!
ANOTHER: That's impossible!

[Metal groans. A low moan rolls over the wall]
[The siren suddenly dies in a burst of static]
[A bright click.]
EZRA (over the system): Hello, Burning Well. I fixed your speakers.
[Static.]
EZRA: To anyone being held in Burning Well against their will: this is
your window. A biter horde is approaching the gates. When you hear the
alarm, move away from the walls and get out while you can.

[Buzzer noise. An alarm sounds]
NORMAN: That's our cue. Cloaks on, now!

35: TO THE STICKING PLACE

The girls raced to the central tower, bumping through the crowd like salmon lurching upstream. Gunfire exploded from the top of the wall and lookout towers.

"The biters got in, I can't believe they got in," breathed Nell as they ducked behind a broken wall. "That was the p-plan," said Jo, craning around the wall to check for an opening.

Something exploded above their heads, showering bits of chalk into their hair.

"They made it sound like that could never happen," said Nell.

"They lie a lot," Jo said.

"Yeah," Nell mumbled. "Yeah, they do, don't they?"

The stench of rotting flesh and decaying wood filled Jo's nostrils. There was murky movement in the corners of Jo's vision, like the edges of a dream.

She caught her first glimpse of a biter emerging through gray smoke. Its flesh was pale and slimy-looking, like a mushroom growing out of wet dirt. The biter's eyes were dark pits, its arms long white roots strangled by dodder curls.

Fox and Rafael must have aroused the deepest part of the valley to unearth the nastiest biters Jo had ever seen. She thought of a fisherman agitating a riverbed.

Jo pulled Nell down a narrow service corridor, past a rack of overturned gurneys and a door hanging loose on one hinge. The floor was slick underfoot. Somewhere farther off, a gun went off and then didn't fire again.

They made it to the medical building, and stopped before going in. A window had shattered, and something scuffled from inside.

Jo slowed, raised her knife, and edged around the corner.

One guard lay sprawled on the floor, blood running into the grout. Another sat slumped against the wall, wrists bound tight with medical tubing, eyes wide and unfocused. Between them, Judee stood braced over a third man, her knee planted between his shoulders as she wrenched his gun free and shoved it into her waistband.

She looked up and took Jo in at a glance.

"Took you long enough."

Judee hauled the man upright, shoved him into a supply closet, and slammed the door shut. Then she turned and waved a cluster of shaken people forward.

Only then did she spare Nell a look. Her mouth twisted.

"You."

Nell flinched and took a step back.

"I—I didn't—"

"Save it," Judee said. She crouched and snapped a lock open with a hairpin she pulled from her sleeve. The door swung wide. Inside, two people stared out, blinking, wrists raw where they'd been bound.

Jo moved to help, and explained the plan as much as she was able, thankful for Judee's quiet efficiency. Jo knelt, worked a second lock with her knife and felt the catch give. A girl's hands grabbed her sleeves, and Jo gently pried them away as the girl sobbed once, then shut her mouth. She went to stand with the rest of the captives.

Judee shoved another door open, checked the corridor, then jerked her chin at Jo.

"Ezra just lit a fire under the whole damn place," she said, as Jo began to dig into her bag for more cloaks. "Which is great and all," Judee continued, "but tell me how we get people out without marching them straight to their deaths, even with those magic cloaks of yours."

The sound of gunfire echoed, growing closer.

"They don't have to be c-calm," Jo said. She had three more cloaks. People would have to squeeze. "They j-just have to move."

Judee reached out to stop Jo's unpacking, dropping her voice.

"We need a safe exit," Judee said. "Some of these folks are hurt bad, and a lot got dragged right out of their communities, their homes. I don't know how calm they'll be walking straight through a horde of them."

Jo stopped what she was doing to look at the others. They were all huddled along the wall, eyes bright and darting. One woman clutched a bandaged knee, a boy sat on the floor with his knees pulled tight, rocking. A man had one eye, and one eye only, which he fixed somewhere beyond the walls of the medical center.

Jo knew that look. They were terrified.

"The g-gate's the only way," Jo said weakly.

Then Nell piped up, small but quick.

"There's a service exit." Judee snapped attention to her.

"Where?"

Nell swallowed.

"Back end of the city. Under the south wall. It's not… it's not meant for people. More like a maintenance grate. You have to crawl, but…"

Jo stared at her. Heat flared in her chest.

"Why didn't you s-say that before?" Nell winced. "You didn't ask! And anyway, nobody ever uses it—"

"Show me where it is," Judee said.

Then, in a burst of inspiration, Jo bent to her boot and pulled out her folded map. The paper was no bigger than her palm, soft from sweat and use. Judee's hand-drawn lines were still there, dark and sure. Jo thrust it at Nell. Then she extracted a pencil from her pack, the one she kept beside her sketchbook.

"Mark it."

Nell's hands shook as she bent over the map and made a small, precise X near the edge of the wall.

Jo snatched the map back and pressed it into Judee's palm, who studied it for half a second. Then Jo handed her the green garments.

"Thanks, kid," said Judee. Her face softened by a fraction. "Don't get yourself killed." Judee led them out, draping one of the cloaks around a few shoulders."

Nell stared.

"You just gave her all of them."

Jo didn't answer. She stood a moment longer, listening to the group of boots retreat. There was a distant roar of something large hitting concrete.

The signal would come. It had to.

Then she tightened her grip on her knife and turned back toward the smoke, the tower, Nell trailing along after her.

A slew of more creatures in various states of decay peeled out of the smoke and whipped their root-like arms around people ten feet away. Jo and Nell watched in horror as the biters descended on any person that ventured too close, tearing limbs off, sinking pointed teeth into necks.

"Why didn't you keep one of those cloaks for us?" Nell asked frantically.

Jo checked to make sure her weapon was loaded and nodded to the center square where the soldiers had scattered in all directions. The stage curtains flapped hole-ridden in the wind. Jo caught a glimpse of bodies slipping away beneath mossy green, vanishing into the churn.

Then, there was movement on the stage and two figures stumbled out from the billowing fabric. A pair of heavy military boots thundered forward and Jo gazed up into the viscous face of General Hayes. He was dragging a frail figure under his massive arm, and in horror Jo realized it was Norman, his glasses dangling off a broken nose. His face glistened with blood.

Jo got up from her hiding spot and barreled towards the stage.

"Are you crazy?" Nell screamed.

Jo felt something sharp whip past her head and graze her scalp. Biters flung themselves into her path. She dodged them and kept running.

She pushed past the mob of audience members, who didn't seem to know whether to run, hide, or watch

"...what we do with traitors!" bellowed General Hayes over the chaos-ridden square.

He raised a blade towards the moon and there were roars of delight, shouts of protest, all mingled with the hum of panic.

Jo ferociously elbowed everyone in her path to get to the stage. Norman's once-distinguished face was turning blue. She aimed her gun between the General's eyes.

He saw her, through her disguise, at her hatless head.

"You," the General mouthed.

Then, a sound rolled in, low and ripping, and the square almost quieted.

Boom.

Drag.

Boom.

Drag.

Two pale lengths rose out of the dark, past the wall, slick and jointed, dragging furrows through concrete as if it were wet soil. The shape hauled itself forward, roots punching down, tearing free, punching down again.

A breath hitched through the crowd. Then the ground split.

The stage buckled as a long white arm burst up through the boards, wood exploding outward. The platform sheared in half with a crack like a tree snapping in a storm.

Norman twisted free as the General staggered. He hit the stage hard and rolled, coughing, as guards lunged and lost their footing on the collapsing planks.

Numb and following her feet by pure instinct, Jo pushed back through the bodies of hysterical people and as fast as she could away from General Hayes' line of sight.

She was so intent on getting away that she almost ran right into a mass of curly yellow dodders. A scream died in Jo's throat as the biter turned to face her. It was twelve feet tall with legs like tree trunks, its face curtained in fungi, it reached out its rotten, scabby hands to grab her.

Jo swung her knife and sliced off the pinky finger, but the biter barely flinched. Unyielding, it advanced with a speed Jo didn't expect as it sunk its fingers into the sleeves of her jacket and brought its gaping mouth towards her throat. She saw a glimmer of bone as it reared its head back and bared a mouth of cluttered teeth.

Jo flung her knife-hand upward with a mere millisecond to spare. The creature's heavy skull hung there on her blade, which she'd sunk into the roof of its mouth. The tip poked out of the creature's eye socket. Jo could have cried with relief, but steeled herself as the creature's dead weight brought her to the ground.

Shaking violently, Jo climbed out from under the clammy body, covered in black goo, and checked her body for cuts or bites, her blood pumping hot through her veins. In awe, she watched in real-time as the yellow dodders that once shone an acid color shriveled on the biter's limbs like singed hair.

She remembered she was still in a town infested with biters, so she found her footing and forced herself forward.

Just get to the tower, she repeated. *Nell has the key. Get the key. Get to the tower. Get Faith. Get the others.*

And then…and then…

Nell was crouched where Jo had left her behind the tool shed, breath coming fast. She was pointing toward the far end of the square, where bodies and smoke churned together.

A tight knot of Wolfskins had formed near the fallen barricade. Sienna stood among them, shouting orders that vanished into the noise. Jo recognized Tom at once with his stiff and crooked stance. One sleeve was dark with blood, but he kept holding the line against the snapping biters.

"Stay together!" Sienna was yelling. "You don't break formation—"

Tom caught himself on the wall, his helmet knocking hard against concrete. For a second, Jo thought he'd just lost his footing. Then he bent forward, hands braced on his knees, and wretched.

As he wiped his mouth, Jo could see a moon-shaped bite on his upper arm, and tangled bits of growth were already forcing their way out. Tom looked down at his own hands and laughed once, like he couldn't believe it. Then his fingers locked, joints seizing as yellow dodder crawled up his forearm and vanished beneath the cuff.

Sienna stopped firing into the smoke, and stared at him.

Tom took a step toward her. Then another. His head jerked sideways, neck cracking, mouth opening wide as his teeth bared. A root punched through his collarbone with a sound like tearing cloth.

Sienna backed away, then she was running. Her boots slipped in the debris, and she disappeared over the wall.

Jo's insides went cold as she watched Tom fall on his hands and knees, biters swarming him now like wasps on sugar.

"What do we do?" Nell whispered, voice hoarse with sobs. "Th-they're everywhere."

They had stayed in one place too long. The horde had come, and Jo had given all her cloaks away. She wondered if he was out there–alive or dead?–among the heads of hungry devourers.

Shivering there with Nell, Jo wracked her brain. They huddled together behind their crate, itching to move, itching to remain.

Then there was movement and Nell yelped. Jo raised her weapon when something grasped her wrist.

"It's me," mouthed Rafael from under the shadow of his cloak.

If ever Jo would have released her weapon from shock, it might have been then. Rafael's square shoulders were draped with foliage like a royal fairy's coat, his dark face smeared with soil, sweat, and grease.

"Get under," he said.

They crawled under the cool folds, Nell whimpering, and Jo kept her close. They began to move, water droplets trickling from the tops of their heads to the base of their necks.

They tiptoed through the throng, knees bent to fit all three. Lush green, yellow, and muddy browns; the stench of rotting flesh and honeysuckle. The horde lurched about, decomposing hands groping for a new host.

Nell made an occasional sound of terror, but shut up quickly when Rafael nudged her. Jo heard the rattling breathing right by her ears, but they were never stopped. They swished gingerly through the horde until they reached the tower at the center of Burning Well.

"Take the way through the servant's quarters," Rafael told them. "You remember how to get to the room, Jo?"

She nodded in the shadow of his arm.

"Good girl," he said, and slipped out from under the cloak, leaving the fabric draped on Nell and Jo's heads. "You'll need that once you get out."

"Raf–"

But he was already yards away, blade glimmering at his side, no garment to protect him from the biters getting a whiff of his scent.

"Fox will keep the Bloomers moving," he said.

He disappeared around the bend.

The tower stood wide and white as bone and blended right into the chalk of the rest of the city. Nell fumbled with something around her neck and extracted a key from the end of a chain.

"You're sure the General has a bunker in there?" Nell said.

"Yes," Jo said.

It satisfied Nell for the moment. The key opened the square servants' door without a hitch.

36: SABOTAGE

The switch clicked back into place and the speakers hissed once before going quiet. Ezra kept his hand on the panel, fingers slick with sweat. The close concrete held the sound of his breathing and sent it back at him.

Somewhere above, something hit the outer wall hard enough to make dust sift down from the ceiling. Ezra wiped his palm on his jeans and grabbed the handheld radio Jo had left him.

It crackled and spat a burst of static. Ezra pressed his ear to the receiver.

"Come on…give me something."

Nothing. Maybe his little signal couldn't reach past the concrete.

Holding the radio aloft, Ezra walked towards the ladder and stood under the hatch, swallowing against the lump in his throat as he imagined it opening and a biter snapping a long root down to snatch him up.

"Focus…" he said, wiping sweat from under his glasses. "Come on…"

"*…repeat…incoming…ates…*"

Ezra slammed the Talk button.

"Rafael? That you?" he whispered as loudly as he dared. "I hope you've got your volume down."

"*…gate is down…they're moving…get out…out…*"

"Get out. Got it. Don't need to tell me twice." Ezra grabbed the ladder with his bandaged hand, then paused. The great beast of a comms center hummed behind him in wait.

He'd spent days on it, fixing the innards and connecting wires, replacing parts, and coaxing sound out of dead speakers. He knew where everything went now.

And he'd stalled for as long as he could. He pretended not to know the mechanics and lied about not having the right parts. It ended when they brought the machete down on his fingers, the ones they said he didn't need.

I was weak, he thought bitterly.

Slipping the cloak around his shoulders—oh, it was heavier than he'd expected, like a wet towel—Ezra approached the beast and gave it one final pat.

"Sorry, girl, " he said. "Can't let the General get his hands on you."

He flipped the power switch *off*. The humming stuttered, rose, then collapsed into a flat, broken whine.

Then he kicked the panel open.

Theo's hands flashed in his head first. He always had dirt under his stubby nails. He remembered late nights hunched over scavenged parts, some video tape crackling on the T.V. as they talked too fast and dreamed too big. Ambridge was theirs.

Ezra yanked a cable free with his bare hands.

He thought of Roslyn and Suncrest. He thought of standing with Jo in the rain, both of them soaked through and lifting the beams that would become the tower. She had braced her shoulder against the post and swore under her breath when it slipped. He liked it when she swore. He liked it when she said anything.

He thought of lying in the grass afterward and splitting apples open with a knife. He thought of the way she'd gone still when she laughed, like the sound surprised her. Her eyes had sparkled like honey in the sunlight.

He thought of the kiss, done because there might not be time for another.

Ezra snapped copper wires, dug out the innards of the machines and cracked them against the floor. Worth it, he decided.

He took up his wrench and smashed the relay box, the board, everything to absolute oblivion.

When there was nothing left that could be salvaged, he stepped back with satisfaction and pulled the hood up over his head. When he stepped into the night, he fully expected Sienna or Tom to appear and knock his head off, but he was quite alone.

Gunsmoke clung to the dirt and tinged the air. Ezra bent his knees and let his shoulders sag under the cloak, the way Jo had told him. He shuffled forward, which wasn't hard to fake.

He clenched his teeth and stared at the breach ahead, dark shapes crawling through the gap in the wall where they'd dragged him in days before. God, he couldn't believe he was moving *towards* it.

"Just…get out," he repeated to himself as biters brushed against his legs. His heart was thudding so hard his ribcage hurt. He wondered if Jo had made it to the tower door.

He touched the frayed edge of the garment. She should have had this, he thought. She was better at this kind of thing.

Something boomed at the wall and the ground shuddered under his feet. A watchtower split with a crack. Its upper half tipped, hung suspended for a breath, then tore loose and crashed out of sight.

Ezra jumped as he heard someone scream from the smoke. A man's scream, guttural and angry. The cry cut short.

Ezra clicked his walkie on.

"Rafael?" he whispered. "Come in. Over." Static hissed back.

The blast had peeled the gateway open wider. As concrete sloughed off in slabs, the dust cleared and the path brightened.

A Bloomer stood in the gathering dust, pale with flowers, its body washed silver by moonlight. Even more Bloomers drifted behind it, heading uphill where they didn't belong.

Ezra stopped short. He'd seen them in the woods near Ambridge, once near Roslyn, but never this many, and never this close. Their bodies shimmered like pale fish underwater as they crossed the broken threshold.

He scanned for cloaks amidst the river of Bloomers. He looked for Rafael. By now, he knew the shape of him from Jo's stories, from the quick charcoal sketch she'd made in Suncrest and folded into her bag. And he knew the voice now.

"Rafael?" he repeated. "Repeat, come in. Please. Over."

A reply came, short and flat. Not Rafael's, but a boy's. A kid's.

"He fell."

Ezra stopped walking.

"Oh," he said, his hand going slack around the radio. *Shit.*

He pictured Jo's face when she talked about Rafael. She said his name like it anchored her.

Ezra swallowed. His mouth opened and nothing useful came out.

"I…shit. Okay," he said finally. "So… now what? Over."

Static breathed in his ear. A Bloomer glided by, so softly Ezra almost felt warmth. Then, *"Phase two."*

37: THE DUKE

The falling gunshots sounded miles away from inside. Jo and Nell stood there for a full minute, soaking in the quiet, in the events that had led them inside the General's house. Jo distinguished the oil paintings adorning otherwise barren walls. They looked like the figures that took up space in Jo's nightmares.

She folded up Rafael's cloak and set it inside her pack, working numbly. She saw his face whenever she blinked. Then she saw Ezra's. Then Judee's. Norman's. She wondered what had happened to Zoe. What about the other players? And Rafael was running around outside without the cloak to mask him.

"Well?" Nell said brusquely, though she made no effort to move away from the door.

A draft curled around Jo's pant leg, blowing in from around the far corner of the hall. She walked forward, Nell following suit.

Nell was uncharacteristically quiet as they turned left at the painting of the sad lady in the orange grove.

They didn't meet anyone along the way. That was almost more concerning.

The stone stairwell dropped steep. The air becoming more stale with every step downward. Jo had her handgun at the ready, Nell close behind, still sniffling.

"A-almost there," Jo said, almost more to herself than her companion.

She wondered if Nell had heard her, or perhaps her stutter and shallow breath was too hard to understand.

But then, Nell replied with a vagueness to her voice,
"What do I do now?"

Jo turned another corner. The walls had narrowed as they stepped down the staircase. Bare concrete replaced painted plaster.

"Hayes won't let me in his precious tower," Nell continued, tripping on a crevice as she dragged her feet. "He didn't want me. I was only here because of…of Sienna." Nell sniffled again, slowing her pace until she dragged a few feet behind Jo. "I can't go anywhere. I'm…I'm useless."

Jo stopped to look at Nell's pale, sunken face. It was with tremendous bewilderment that Jo realized she actually felt a little sorry for her.

Against her better judgment, Jo said, "Ambridge is g-good."

Nell *tsked.*

"No, thanks," she said. Then added, "They wouldn't let me."

Jo shrugged.

"They let me."

They didn't speak again until they reached the bottom floor.

The corridor opened into a low, wide chamber carved straight from concrete. Cots lined the walls. Blankets lay heaped where people had been told to wait.

Eight women pressed together against the far wall, backs to stacks of crates and medical bins. Behind them stood a thick steel bunker door set into the concrete, round wheel at its center, shut tight. There was no handle on their side.

"Who's there?" one said.

"Who's that?" "Biters?" another whispered.

The brides were draped in linens, all beautiful, and all shaken. Faith stood in front, defiance in her bright eyes. She looked thin, and Jo realized that Faith must have given birth in the months they'd been apart. It felt like a lifetime ago.

Faith was gripping something in both hands. Upon closer inspection, Jo could see it was a chair leg.

Faith squinted through the darkness, and dropped the tip of her weapon.

"Johanna?"

Jo took in the faces: Faith, Washington, and Billie, her belly rounded beneath a thin wrap. And others she didn't know. One woman stood slightly apart from the rest, tall and spare, dark eyes set deep under straight black hair pulled back tight. She held herself the way Fox did, alert even at rest.

"It can't be Rafael's ward," someone gasped.

"What are you doing back here?" said Billie.

Jo's chest swelled with emotion but she stood solid as she gazed around at old and new faces.

"Gonna g-get you out," she said.

Faith rushed forward to grasp Jo by the shoulders. Her face looked raw from crying.

"They took the babies down there," she said, gesturing to the vault. "And the nursemaids. The door won't budge."

Jo went to the vault door and grabbed the wheel. It didn't budge, swollen with humidity. She grit her teeth and felt her muscles twinge.

"C-come on," Jo growled, nodding her head as the other brides looked on. "Together."

Thin hands flew to help and yanked in unison. Faith wedged her chair leg between the spokes of the wheel and the wall, throwing all her weight downwards.

The metal gave a whine, and the door shifted a fraction. They hauled again.

There was pressure from the other side as the nursemaids pushed and shoved with all their might. At last the vault flew open and slammed against the wall with a deafening bang.

Jo waved them through.

"G-get them," she hissed.

The nursemaids stumbled out first, arms full of round and clean babies, wrapped tight in fresh cloth. The infants blinked at the sudden brightness. They were no older than a year, but most of them were smaller. Each woman took a child and held them close to her chest. Some tied quick slings across their shoulders in practiced knots.

Faith stepped forward and took a baby from a nursemaid, and the child cried loud and thin. Faith pulled the sling across her own shoulder, settled the baby against her front, and pressed her cheek to the downy head. The crying softened to hiccups.

As Jo moved them back towards the staircase, another door on the far side of the chamber creaked open.

General Hayes stepped out of the crack of the door, his face streaked with soot and blood. He froze when he saw the vault opened, when he saw Jo.

Fury rose in Jo's throat and burned there. She wanted to bore a hole in his head with her stare, wanted to tear the look of surprise off his face with her bare hands. She stepped in front of the others and raised her gun with both hands.

Hayes's hand flashed to his belt and came up with a pistol leveled at Jo's chest.

"You don't take them," he said. "Those children stay here."

"They're n-not yours."

His lip curled.

"She speaks," he said in mock wonder. "They are the last future I have, Johanna," he continued. "The last future *we all* have."

Behind Jo, someone choked back a sob. There was a stubborn shuffle towards the steps.

"If you pull that trigger," Hayes said, and swung his pistol past Jo, sighting down the line of women and children, "you kill them yourself."

She calculated. If she fired and missed, the round would skip off the close walls and tear through whoever stood behind her.

Jo stepped into the path of the barrel. He did not look as tall as he once was. And whatever happened, if he killed her, at least she would die standing up.

"One last chance to move, little Johanna," said Hayes.

"No."

Suddenly, something struck him from the side.

"Wha—?!"

He buckled as Faith brought the broken chair leg down again. Something cracked—either bone or wood, Jo wasn't sure which—and the gun flew out of Hayes' hand.

He hit his knees, stunned, and the women fell on him all at once.

Both bride and nursemaid descended on Hayes like a pack of lionesses, hammering his skull with their fists, tearing his hair with their nails and ripping at every bit of flesh they could reach. Baby in one arm and the chair leg in the other, Faith hammered his ribs.

He howled and twisted loose, dragging himself across the concrete toward the bunker door. The women tore his coat as he hauled himself inside and the steel door slammed shut. The wheel spun with a hard metallic grind and struck, locked.

Before anyone could celebrate, a groan rolled up through the floor and through the soles of Jo's boots.

Dust sifted from the ceiling in a little snowfall. The concrete beneath her feet flexed.

Jo turned on the others, her limbs going numb.

"Up," she said, voice raw. "Hurry."

They stumbled to obey, with babies fussing all the way up the stairs. Faith passed with the baby strapped tight across her chest, face streaked with tears and grit. Jo and Nell stayed on the ground floor, helping the others up until only a few remained.

Behind them, a thin crack split the concrete, and Jo felt it in her teeth. The jagged line raced across the chamber and cracked under the vault door, which shuddered.

"What *is* that?" Nell coughed.

Inside the vault, there was a muffled thud. Then another.

Jo pictured white roots boring through steel, thick growth forcing its way into every seam, nothing to stop it once it found a way through. She knew they'd be seeing roots any moment if they didn't flee.

"Move!" she shouted again, driving the last cluster toward the steps.

Billie stumbled, one hand locked around the strap at her belly, the other reaching back. Washington caught her elbow and hauled her upright.

The floor split wider.

A second limb punched through, jointless and slick, blindly groping for purchase. It struck the ground hard, dragging a furrow through the concrete as it swept toward the stairs. The limb caught Washington across the back of the thigh and tore through fabric and flesh in one brutal pull. She went down with a cry that cut short as Jo grabbed her under the arms and dragged.

"Leave me," Washington gasped, fingers clawing uselessly at the floor.

"No," Jo said, teeth bared as she pulled. Not another one. Not one more. Another crack sounded overhead, and dust rained down.

Nell grabbed Washington's other arm, and together, they hauled her the last few feet. Washington's leg bent wrong beneath her, blood slicking the steps as Billie turned back, sobbing, trying to help while her baby wailed.

Jo shoved from behind until they cleared the turn in the stairwell. The white limb slammed into the wall where they'd been seconds before, stone exploding outward in a spray that stung Jo's neck and hands.

Below them, Hayes was still screaming. When everyone had made it to the top, Jo burst through the stairwell door and slammed it shut.

The hallway beyond was narrow and bare, quiet except the muffled violence below their feet. There was some murmuring, some whispered prayers, but Faith gently shushed them as Jo squinted into the darkness.

"That's it," Nell said hoarsely. She pointed to a dim square at the end of the hall. "That's the exit."

Jo led them to the door, hands steady despite the shake in her arms. She slid the latch free and pushed the door open a fraction at a time.

Biters. Everywhere. They moved almost in slow-motion, their leafy heads lolling to the sides so their toothy mouths hung agape.

"Come back here!" Faith hissed as Jo stepped down the first step like she was testing the weather.

The biters moved in aimless fashion, almost drunkenly. A biter shuffled close enough that she could see the patch still sewn to its jacket sleeve. Wolfskin. Her stomach knotted, one hand on her pistol. But it veered past her shoulder and kept going, drawn by nothing she could see. Around them, the horde wandered, unfocused, as if something just beyond the street had their attention instead.

Then, one of the figures broke apart from the rest, and this one had color in his cheeks and stray leaves in his curly hair.

Ezra limped towards her, right through the swarm in his heavy cloak. He adjusted his cracked glasses and said,

"Hey, there."

Jo reached and caught his arm, steadying him, and herself.

Behind him, two other figures peeled out of the swarm. One was Fox, and beside him, who stood a few heads taller, a Bloomer. A bouquet of petals cascaded from its head and shoulders as it picked its way through ash with bone-thin legs. Up close, Jo could pick out tender buds peppering the spaces between its ribs. It looked more like an old monument than a person.

More Bloomers followed, pooling out of the breach in the wall and gaps in the street, from behind fallen pillars. They drifted forward, the current of biters making space.

The women stood at the entrance to the tower, stiff and unbelieving. The air, which was clouded with dust just hours before, was clear and crisp-looking, tiny golden particles twinkling like fireflies.

"Ready to go?" Ezra asked, extending his hand. Jo took it.

The Bloomers closed around them, soft as a breeze. It was under the cover of the canopy and the quiet of the night that they left the ashes of Burning Well together.

IV: JOURNEY'S END

38: IN LOVERS' MEETING

It was raining in Ambridge, and Bloomers loved the rain.

There was at least one on every corner of the garden: the raised vegetable beds and herbs, the straight rows of corn, the shiny fruit-laden trees. But the Bloomers liked the flowerbeds most. The riot of colors, from azure to scarlet, attracted all sorts of pollinators and turned the Bloomers into creatures worthy of their name. They'd stand still for days at a time like botanical statues, butterflies flitting lazily around their heads. To the untrained eye, the gentle things were nothing more than trees, and there had not been one singular biter incident since the flowery-headed creatures had moved into town.

Jo dug her hands into the black soil and brushed off another long carrot before dropping it in the bucket. Rainwater dripped off her nose, so she raised her hood and inhaled the sweet, irony scent of the earth. It was good to get her hands dirty.

Faith trumped over to Jo's spot and dumped her own harvest into the quickly filling bucket.

Billie wrenched her sopping hair off her neck and stuffed it under her rain hat.

"Can we be done?" she asked grumpily.

"Already?" Faith teased, leaning her head back to feel the cool drops on her ruddy skin. The baby strapped to her chest cooed and waved his little arms as though trying to catch a raindrop. "But it smells amazing out here."

"My socks are wet," Billie complained.

"Cooooome in, Crow, this is Prophet. What's the status of your arrival? I'm having a little trouble mixing the paint like you showed me. Over."

Jo wiped her muddy hands on her pant legs and picked up the walkie-talkie.

"Hi," she said into the radio. Faith gave her a suggestive little wink, to which Jo shoved her playfully aside.

"Oh, I'm sorry, I can't hear you," said Ezra. *"Because someone didn't identify themselves, and I can't in good conscience continue an encrypted conversation without the reassurance that this person, whoever she is, is who I need to talk to. And this person also didn't say 'over'. Over."*

Jo sighed and clicked the 'Talk' button.

"This is Crow. Obviously. Over."

"Oh, well, hi back. Gosh, it's good to hear from you. How's the gardening going? Over."

"Good," said Jo.

"Cold," grumped Billie into the speaker.

"Ah, well, Spring gets cold sometimes," Ezra said unhelpfully. *"Crazy how fast stuff's been growing, huh? Over."*

It was true: their beds were bursting with life and producing crops nearly every week: carrots, potatoes, corn, green beans, medicinal herbs, mushrooms. Ambridge was surrounded with trees that had never bore fruit before the Bloomers moved in, and now the branches were bursting with oranges and apples, lemons and figs.

Jo stood to stretch, and hauled up her bucketful of vegetables.

"Gonna d-drop off at the storehouse," she said, slipping by a docile Bloomer, admiring the new stalk growing along the bone like it was a trellis. "And I'll m-meet you at comms. Over."

"Okay, heard. I get it. You're a busy woman. Just thought you'd fancy a chat while you're working, but I can see now that I'm nothing more than a mosquito in your ear. I'll just talk to you when you get here. I'm not lonely. Or missing you. So there. Over and out, for now. Just get here quick, please, before the paint dries."

Jo waved to her fellow harvesters and left the gardens. She stepped under the stone archway and splashed down the path back to Ambridge. She stopped by the storehouse and heaved her bucket of crops on the counter.

"You get the ginger?" asked Nell, frowning as she shoved her hand into the bucket.

"Mhm," Jo said. She didn't mention that the roots were sitting at the very bottom of the bucket, under ten pounds of carrots.

Nell's blonde hair had grown past her chin, thicker than Jo had ever seen it. The ends were tinged with dirt.

"I keep telling you to put the herbs on *top* of the other crops or just use another bucket. You keep crushing them, and I don't know what to tell Judee when she needs ginger for tonics."

"Ginger's a root," Jo countered. "Strong."

Nell picked the carrots out one by one and lined them up on the counter.

"Just get *two* buckets next time. Geez. I have to do everything around here."

Jo pulled her hood up to brave the rain once more. She had one more stop to make.

The stone archway rose at the edge of the path, whitewashed against the green. Rain tapped softly at the ground beneath it, carrying the clean smell of wet earth. Jo slowed as she approached. Up close, the stone showed its age. Every block bore a name, carved by different hands at different times. Some letters were neat and others wavered, but all of them had been cut deep.

She traced the curve of the arch with her palm, then let her hand fall to the wall beside it. Her fingers moved over the grooves until they found what they were looking for.

Rafael.

The stone was cool under her skin. The letters were rough, the edges still sharp. She pressed her thumb into the carving and held it there. Rain slid down her sleeve.

Her throat tightened. She swallowed, once, then again, and stayed where she was until the feeling eased. When she finally stepped back, she left her handprint dark on the stone.

The rain lightened as Jo made her way up the hill, her lungs full with exercise, and she arrived at the radio tower. She noted the new *Apocalypse Train* flag flapping in the breeze in bright blue. As she walked along the outside of the old wood shack, she found a lanky boy leaning on his cane, scowling deeply at the wall. He had smears of blue and yellow paint on his clothes and hands. But as she approached and he turned to face her, he was bright and beaming.

"Come see," he said, and Jo jogged up beside him and faced the comms center.

The mural on the side was still in-progress—a project Jo had dreamed up and Ezra helped with, though he claimed not to have an artistic bone in his body.

"I added some names at the bottom, in case we need to keep, uh, adding to it," he said. "What do you think?"

Jo tilted her head to one side and studied the familiar faces on the wall: Theo's crooked smile, Birdie's dignified expression, Ruth's dark eyes, and Rafael's stoic face, among many others lost along the way. It was a crowded mural, but somehow it worked, with every person connected by lush flowers, which Jo would not have known how to paint if it hadn't been for the populous of bloomers.

"I love it," Jo said honestly.

"Great!" Ezra said. "Also, just got word from Suncrest: Zoe says they're doing *Winter's Tale* next. You read that one?"

"Nope," Jo said, following his long strides to take shelter under the roof. The rain was falling hard again.

"We'll have to take another trip to the library," Ezra mused, shaking his head and spraying Jo with water. "Which works out great, since—oh! I didn't tell you! Earth-shattering news, actually—apparently, someone dropped off a VHS box set of that missing *Gilmore Girls* season! Can you believe it? After all these years. And what's great is that those old VHS tapes are notoriously sturdy, so there's a good chance we'll finally get to see what happens with our favorite diner boy and coffee lady."

Jo smiled.

"Theo would've liked that."

"Yeah. Yeah, I think so," Ezra said, going a little quiet. "Gotta hand it to him, the *Gilmore Girls* segment is our most popular one on the show. How annoying is that? So I guess that means we gotta keep the recap going. Not that you have to do the show with me, but if you want to keep watching, hey, I'd love it.

"You don't have to talk if you don't want to. I just like it when you're here. With me. Here with me." Ezra ran a hand through his curls. "Ha-ha, sheesh, cheesy much? I'll answer for you: yes. Cheesy much."

Jo took his hand and under the music of the rain, kissed him. It was a gloriously boring afternoon.

ACKNOWLEDGMENTS

Thank you to my directors, professors, mentors, fellow actors and friends throughout my theatre education and training. This book was born from my own healing that came with art and connection to others. Theatre was, and continues to be, my safe place (my library), where healing happens. I'm so grateful.

An eternal thank-you to God, for restoring what was broken, for teaching me how to listen, and for calling me toward connection when I would have chosen silence.

My gratitude to the badass team at Ink & Quill Press, who championed this hodge-podge of a debut with so much enthusiasm and care.

I have to thank my developmental editor Melinda Crouchley, who helped me in the early drafts and nudged me not to give up on this story.

Thanks also to my first readers: Faith, Claire, and the roommates at Big Blue, who crafted a space of stories, love, and fun while this book was in its messiest stages. Kelsey, Sydney, Haley. And to Abigail and Amber, my wildest cheerleaders. Thank you all.

To all the friends who have shown up time and time again to encourage my writings (even when they consist of me reading the Twilight books simply because they're my current fixation), who use real, actual money to buy my books and support all the things I make: D, Kevin, Danny. Love you all. Iska, my Other Evil Stepsister, who ignited my love of storytelling all the way back in high school and my always-there friend; and Yared, for always lending expertise, book recs, and support to everything I write, even when it's super rough.

All the gratitude in the world to my mama, who cultivated a house of art, love, and creativity, who is my most wonderful inspiration, teacher, and friend. To my pop, always a pillar of strength and love, always there with a bear hug, and who played the Scar to my Simba when I was three. That's probably why I'm the best actor anyone's ever seen, I think. Beeg hug, leetle kees.

And finally, the most special thanks to my oh-so-talented and most loving husband; my whetstone, my greatest encourager, my love in the time of the apocalypse, and a thousand more complimentary metaphors. And for good measure, here's one more: thank you for being my lamplighter, for helping me to hope, love, and be loved when things get too dark.

LYDIA JOY is a writer and illustrator based in Colorado. She is the author of *Love & Radio in the Time of the Apocalypse* and *The First Draft Handbook* and has illustrated books including *Feels Like Home* by Kelsey French.

She is also the creator of the webcomics *The Hobby Goblin* and Wallflowers on Webtoon.

When she's not writing or drawing, she can usually be found painting, making zines, reading in the corner of a local coffee shop, watering her plants, or cooking and playing D&D with her husband.

Lydia received her Bachelor's degree in Theatre Arts from the University of Northern Colorado.

--

Find more of her work at www.lydiajoyportfolio.com and www.lydiajoytheartist.substack.com

Follow on socials @lydiajoy.inks